BARN BOOT BLUES

BY
CATHERINE FRIEND

AMAZON CHILDREN'S PUBLISHING

Library of Congress Cataloging-in-Publication Data

Friend, Catherine.
Barn boot blues / by Catherine Friend. — 1st ed.
p. cm.
Summary: When her parents swap urban life in Minneapolis for rural life on a farm 100 miles away, twelve-year-old Taylor feels as if she is living on another planet.
ISBN 978-0-7614-5827-2 (hardcover) — ISBN 978-0-7614-5930-9 (ebook)
[1. Farm life--Minnesota—Fiction. 2. Minnesota—Fiction.] I. Title.
PZ7.F91523Bar 2011
[Fic]—dc22
2011001909

Book design by Alex Ferrari
Editor: Margery Cuyler

Printed in the United States of America (R)
First edition
10 9 8 7 6 5 4 3

For Melissa

CHAPTER ONE

MY NAME IS TAYLOR McNAMARA. I LIKE TO SHOP AND watch TV and hang out with friends. I'm twelve. I'm an excellent student.

I'm also discombobulated.

This is a great word, but it's not really a great feeling. It means everything's off balance. Your life feels weird. It's what happens when, in the middle of August, your parents pack your entire life into cardboard boxes and hire Two Guys With a Truck to remove those boxes from your house in Minneapolis (population 400,000.) Then Two Guys With a Truck unload the boxes into an old farmhouse one hundred miles away. The closest town is Melberg (population 7,380.) One day my world is full of people and the Mall of America and Lucinda's Pizza Parlor. The next day my world is a farm (population 77—forty chickens, twenty sheep, ten ducks, four goats, and three humans).

See what I mean? Discombobulating.

I'm determined, though, not to *stay* discombobulated. To become *un*discombobulated, I must make new friends, figure out how to fit into a new school and a new town, and learn about sheep, goats, ducks, and chickens. What could be so hard about that? (Another thing about me. When I feel discombobulated, I get sarcastic. Mom and Dad hate that, even though they have a parenting book that says sarcasm begins at twelve. I'm right on schedule.)

Because my parents are excited to be new farmers, it's too bad I'm not more excited to be a farm *kid*. But since I've only been one for three weeks, I might need more practice. Right now I'm waiting for the bus on the first day of school. My entire world is a gravel road, two friendly cows in Mr. Benson's pasture across the road, and a little house on the driveway next to me. Dad says people in the country built these little shelters to protect kids from the wind as they waited for the school bus. The shelter has a roof and windows and flower boxes, but it's only big enough for two people. The paint's peeling, the door's missing, and the whole thing's sagging toward the ditch.

I inspect my clothes. I'm wearing my favorite green top. I picked it because it makes my green eyes pop like emeralds. "Hey, cows, how do I look?" One of them moos through a mouthful of grass, which makes me laugh. Then she turns away and poops—splat!—onto the grass. Maybe she thinks I should wear a different top.

I wipe my hands on my denim skirt. Will anyone sit with me at lunch? Will I have nice teachers or strict ones? This is a small town. Will I know what to say to people? What if I say the wrong thing?

I jump when the screen door slams. "I'm late!" Mom calls as she runs toward the garage, her light brown ponytail streaking behind her. She's starting a part-time job at the Melberg Grain Elevator. It's a place where farmers buy corn and other grain for their animals to eat. When Mom backs the car out of the garage, gravel spins under the tires.

"Late for work!" She reaches through the open window for a hug. "Relax, Tay, you'll be fine. Everyone will love you, just like at your old school. Did you collect eggs this morning?"

I smack my forehead. "I forgot. Mom, I've had so much to think about."

Mom checks her watch. "The bus won't come for another ten minutes. You have time. An egg could break during the day and make a mess. Love you!" And she disappears down the road in a cloud of white dust.

I look at the chicken house. I look at my clean pink sandals. Erk. I drop my backpack and run for the house. Inside the front door, our barn boots are lined up along the wall. Dad's are black, Mom's are forest green, and mine are mud brown, the only color available in my size. The hard rubber squeaks as I slide my feet inside. The high boots slap against my calves as I clomp outside to the chicken house. I try walking normally, but I still sound like a horse.

The chicken house is a long narrow building with no paint left and half the roof shingles missing. Chickens peck at the ground and coo. I like the sound they make, but I could do without the white, slimy poop. Mom says I should call it manure, but I'm sorry. Whether it comes out of a cow or a sheep or a chicken, it's poop.

Inside the chicken house, I grab the mesh basket and begin hunting for eggs in the nest boxes nailed to the wall. Luckily the hens are outside eating bugs, so I can gather eggs without getting hurt. The first day that I collected eggs, the hens were sitting in the nest boxes and pecked my wrist. I wore a bracelet of scabs for a week.

I find fifteen eggs. They are smooth and all different shapes. One looks like a bullet, another is nearly perfectly round. One is so big there must be two yolks inside. Some eggs are light brown, some white, but my favorites are the soft blue and light green eggs. Amazing. I reach the last box and discover Butterscotch, her gold feathers gleaming like candy. She's the only hen that likes me.

I stroke her and she fluffs up and makes a low sound in her throat, but she doesn't peck me. Her feathers are silky soft. She makes the throat sound again. I should record it and send it to my best friend Lauren back in Minneapolis.

Lauren. She'll be seeing all of our friends today. Every single person I know goes to a school that's one hundred miles away. I sigh heavily.

Suddenly the ground trembles and the window in the chicken house rattles. The vibrations grow worse. The bus! It's early!

I stash the basket of eggs in the little fridge, then flee the chicken house and race down the driveway. Luckily the driver sees me and slows down. I grab my backpack, jump on the bus, and take the first empty seat, scooting toward the window. My heart pounds in my ears. I gasp, trying to catch my breath. The bus smells of shampoo and brand-new backpacks.

Trying to appear calm, I curl my sweaty toes inside my boots.

Boots. I look down. No! Erk, erk, *erk!*

The bus buzzes with voices. Two boys sitting behind me begin to whisper and laugh.

My face catches on fire. They're laughing at me.

I am twelve. I am living on a farm. I am on my way to a new school wearing ugly barn boots. No wonder I'm discombobulated.

CHAPTER TWO

ONE OF THE BOYS SITTING BEHIND ME LEANS FORWARD. "Nice boots," he says with a smirk. "Totally hot." That sets them laughing again.

"Very funny," I mutter. A small pain starts forming behind my eyes.

I reach for my MP3 player as a girl slides into the seat beside me. "Josh, stop being such a jerk." It's our neighbor, Caleigh. Mom introduced me to Caleigh and Mrs. Kyllo in the grocery store last weekend. Caleigh's tall, and her curly brown hair sticks out from under the Larsen's Feed cap jammed on her head. "Ignore Josh. He's studying to be a human but keeps failing the test."

She flashes me a wide smile, but I'm still too embarrassed about the boots to return it. Then she looks down at my feet. "The bus came earlier than you thought it would, didn't it."

Someone who understands! Maybe some of the other kids will too. I shuffle my feet, as if that will make the boots disappear. "I was collecting eggs and petting Butterscotch when the bus came."

"You name your hens?"

My mind spins. Is that a bad thing? A good thing? "Just one of them."

"We used to name ours, too, but hens don't live that long. If they have names, it's easier to get attached to them, and then it's sadder when they die. It's also hard to eat something with a name."

My eyes widen. I'd never thought about that. Will Mom or Dad one day serve me Butterscotch chicken soup?

"How are your sheep?" Caleigh asks. "I love sheep, but Dad won't let me get any."

"I guess they're okay."

Josh guffaws behind us. "Boots raises sheep?"

I turn to face Josh, marveling at his long eyelashes. My jaw tightens. "Don't call me Boots."

He grins. "Hey, what's the only thing dumber than a sheep?" He elbows the boy next to him. "The farmer that raises 'em."

"Very funny," I snap, whirling around to face the front of the bus.

"Ignore him," Caleigh says. "So, how many bucks do you have?"

I swallow. How many bucks *do* we have? My parents don't discuss money with me. I take a deep breath and let it out. "How many bucks does one farm really need?"

Caleigh shudders. "Only one, of course. They smell so terrible that some days *one* is too many. I don't know how you can stand it."

Oh! Buck. Male goat. "I can't," I say. "Jersey stinks like a dumpster."

The school bus reaches Melberg and drives through a neighborhood with three-story houses perched on each corner of the block. We pass my favorite, the house I noticed when Mom and Dad first gave me a tour of Melberg. It's light blue and has burgundy trim with soft pink highlights running along the roof and porch. Mom says it's a Queen Ann-style house, but it looks like a castle. When I grow sad about living in our rundown farmhouse with its moldy basement and rippling kitchen floor and water-stained ceilings, I imagine living in one of those turrets.

A girl my age comes out the front door and waves to someone inside. Her long black hair sways as she walks, and she's wearing a blue suede skirt and matching sandals. I doubt there is chicken poop on the bottom of *her* footwear. She climbs on the bus and walks to the back.

Five minutes later the bus squeals to a stop in front of the Melberg Middle School, an old two-story brick building.

"Here we are," Caleigh announces.

I hurry off the bus and push through the crowd before Josh can tease me again. Maybe no one will notice the boots. The hallways are dark and narrow, lined with battered tan lockers. The walls are plastered with self-esteem posters and sports schedules. When Mom registered me last week, I was assigned a locker, given my class schedule, and introduced to the principal, Mr. Maybourne.

I stash my pack in my locker, find my way to Room 135, and take the first empty seat. The girl behind me smiles. "I love your skirt, but will it pass the Maybourne Test?"

"The what?"

The tall man standing at the front of the room taps his desk with a ruler to get our attention. When everyone is quiet, he says, "My name is Mr. Suarez, and I'll be your teacher for Team Time. Every morning I'll take attendance and hand out information about school activities." He considers the list on his clipboard, looks around the room, and starts checking off names. It turns out the girl behind me is named Portia.

After he finishes taking attendance, he tosses the clipboard onto his desk and nods. "Good. Everyone's here this morning. We also have a new student. Taylor, why don't you stand, tell us your name, and share something about yourself."

I slowly rise and try to imagine I am calm instead of nervous. "My name's Taylor McNamara. I moved here from Minneapolis three weeks ago. My parents bought a farm from Mrs. Sommers, and they bought all her animals, too. I like soccer and shopping and reading. I don't know anything about animals. It's really weird living out in the country. It's too quiet." My brain knows that my mouth should stop talking, but I can't. "We have sheep and goats and chickens and some little baby ducks. I like the baby ducks the best. I don't like the goats. Yesterday I had to hold

one of the goats while my mom cut open a cyst on its leg."
I gasp for breath. "Gross, totally gross. Maybe I'll stop talking now before I actually describe it."

The class laughs and my face grows warm. In a situation like this, Lauren would blush, but I blotch. I get hot,
and red patches appear and disappear across my neck and
face.

Mr. Suarez's eyes are kind. "Yes, cysts might fall under
the category of Too Much Information." He glances at my
boots and one eyebrow shoots up.

I lick my lips. Think fast! Think clever! "These are a
mistake," I say, "one I won't make again. It's like wearing
two ovens."

Everyone laughs and I blotch again, relieved. It's better
to have the class laughing with me than at me. My insides
feel shaky but I manage to close my mouth and sit down.

"Well, welcome, Taylor McNamara. We're glad you're
here." He reaches for a stack of black notebooks. "I'm going
to hand out this year's student planners. Carry your planners with you at all times and use them to keep track of
your homework assignments and school activities. Also, any
demerits, tardies, times you're caught in the hall without a
pass, dress code violations, and other behavioral problems
will be recorded by a teacher or by Mr. Maybourne. You
must show your planner to your parents every weekend and
have them sign it. Monday mornings, I'll check your planners to make sure you've all done this."

My face cools down as everyone focuses on the planners, not on me. I flip through mine, hardly looking at the section for demerits. I'm not worried about these, or about tardies or dress code violations, since I'm not one of those kinds of kids. I always do the right thing. I always behave. After today, I will fade into the crowd. I will fit in and everything will be fine.

CHAPTER THREE

English and math go well. Kids smile at me, and between classes Caleigh says "hi" in the hallway. Still, I feel stupid in my boots, so after Second Period, I dash out of the room, pushing past the slower-moving students, and hurry down the hall, determined to be the first to get to science. Ten black lab tables take up most of the room. I hurry to the very back table and hop up onto a stool, tucking my boots beneath me so no one will notice them.

Kids start coming in. Josh and another guy head to my table. I moan. It's just my luck that Josh is in both my math *and* science classes.

"Hey, Boots. Bad news. You're sitting at our table."

There are no names on the tables. "Sorry, but I was here first." It bugs me when boys think they own things that they really don't. It bugs me when boys think they can intimidate a new girl into moving to a different table.

Josh's eyes narrow. "Look, Boots, you're new, so here's some advice: Find another table."

Heart pounding, I lean closer. "First, don't call me Boots. Second, get used to disappointment. It'll make failing science so much easier."

"Wow. Someone who stands up to Josh Magnuson? Sweet." The girl from the castle walks up to my table.

Josh snorts. "Forget it." He and his friend move.

"I love your top," the girl gushes. "It's green, like your eyes."

I feel shy, but I thank her.

"You must be the new girl. I'm Megan Zink."

"Taylor McNamara." I take a deep breath. "I'm taking applications for friends, since I'm new here. Interested?"

"Hmmm. Okay, who was the best dressed actress at the Emmys?"

I'd watched the Emmys at home, at my *real* home, last winter. "Christina Cho."

"And the worst?"

"Monica Storm."

"Totally. What's your favorite TV show?"

"Celebrity Star Stage."

Megan squeals softly. "Awesome. The suspense last night nearly killed me. Who do you think is going to win this year?"

I can't bluff my way through an answer because I have no idea who the contestants are. "I couldn't watch it. We don't have TV reception."

"What?"

"My parents think my mind will expand more without electronics. No cable, no satellite dish, no TV."

"That's awful. Where do you live?"

"My parents bought a farm. Sheep, goats, chickens, and ducks."

Megan's eyes narrow. "Do you like living on a farm?"

I shrug. "My parents keep telling me I need to give it more time, but everything feels . . . No, not really."

"Welcome to my list of friends," Megan says.

My next step is risky, but what do I have to lose? "As your first official duty, could you help me with these?" I step out from behind the table and point to my boots.

Megan's mouth drops open. "Wow."

"The school bus came before I could change into my sandals after collecting eggs. You wouldn't have an extra pair of sandals in your locker, would you?"

"I'm so sorry, I don't. Wow," she says again.

Mr. Rashid finally arrives, muttering something about a meeting running late, so after giving me a brilliant smile, Megan takes a seat near the front of the room.

Before Mr. Rashid gets too far into telling us what we're going to learn this year, a short, plump man, bald as a soccer ball, knocks on the open door. It's Mr. Maybourne, the principal.

"Good morning, everyone." He strides into the room, clasping his thick hands together. "I'd like to welcome everyone. You're going to have a fine year, and I'm confident you'll learn a great deal and have fun doing it." He scans the room. "I recognize nearly everyone here, so welcome back. Has everyone met our new student, Taylor McNamara?"

Unfortunately, Mr. Maybourne is one of those principals who likes to shake students' hands, so he walks toward me, hand held out. I have no choice but to step from behind the lab table and shake his hand. When I do this, he squints at my skirt. "It's good to have you with us, Taylor, but I'm concerned about the length of your skirt. Did you read the Melberg Student Handbook?"

I shake my head.

"Could you please put your hands down at your sides?" The other kids gasp, like they know what's coming. When I do, he frowns at my skirt. "Just as I thought. Your skirt is above regulation length."

"Regulation length?" My breath catches in my throat.

"A skirt must be a full one inch longer than your fingertips." I stare down at my hands. The skirt is right at my fingertips. This must be the Maybourne Test that Portia mentioned.

"Mr. Maybourne, I've seen lots of skirts today that are this short."

More gasps. You'd think I'd announced I'd murdered someone. I want to melt into a puddle.

"Your planner, please." After I hand it to him, Mr. Maybourne scrawls a note in thick Sharpie on the Demerits page. Erk! My first day and already I have a demerit. I can't believe it.

"Please get a pass from Mr. Rashid and go to the office.

Mrs. Kozmicki will give you a pair of sweatpants from the Lost and Found."

As I walk to the front of the room, thirty pairs of eyes burn holes in my back.

CHAPTER FOUR

THE OFFICE IS JUST DOWN THE HALL, BUT BECAUSE IT'S the first day of school, the Lost and Found box is empty. "Could you please tell Mr. Maybourne that there are no clothes here?" I say to Mrs. Kozmicki. The last thing I need is for the principal to give me a demerit every time he sees me.

I return to science class. Everyone stares at my skirt, including Mr. Rashid. I explain the problem and he waves me back to my table. Megan grins. "Lucky you," she whispers as I pass.

I nod, stunned. This day isn't going as well as I'd hoped. How many other rules will I break before the day ends?

Lunch isn't fun because I don't know anyone. I search for Megan or Caleigh but can't find either of them. I sit alone at the end of a long table. In the afternoon, two more teachers scold me about my skirt, but I explain about the empty Lost and Found before they go demerit crazy on me. My old school had a dress code, but no one enforced it unless a student showed up wearing something scary like a shirt with a gun on it.

After the last bell I stop at my locker to pick up my backpack, fill it with the textbooks I need, and head for the bus. Outside, a bunch of girls are standing on the sidewalk. Everyone claps. Megan bursts from the crowd and runs toward me. I blotch like crazy. She throws her arms around me and the other girls pat my shoulders and arms. "You did it!" Megan says. I look as confused as I feel. "You set a school record. Absolutely no one who flunks Maybourne's test has worn her skirt all day. We all end up in ugly sweatpants."

The girls around me smile. "But to wear a skirt on the first day?" one girl says. "When there's nothing in the Lost and Found box? Awesome."

They escort me to the bus and I climb on. This is a wacky, wacky school. The whole way home, I text Lauren about my day in brown barn boots and a too-short denim skirt.

Lauren texts back all the news—Charmayne lost ten pounds, Ashley gained ten, Sarah Ann hates Lauren. Lauren hates Jessica, so Jessica and Sarah Ann are now best friends. Mr. Marcus shaved off his beard. Ms. Hartford is now Ms. Brehmer. By the time I read all of Lauren's texts, I'm not only homesick, I'm school sick and friend sick.

CHAPTER FIVE

I WALK DOWN OUR SHORT DRIVEWAY AFTER THE BUS DROPS me off. The old farmhouse, its white paint peeling like a bad sunburn, is on my left. Next to the house is a beaten-down garage with two doors, one permanently stuck open. To the right is the chicken house, and next to that is an ancient barn. It must have been red once, but now it's so faded it looks pinkish-gray in the sun. Behind the barn, the land slopes down to a huge sheep pasture.

Dad isn't home. He's still in Minneapolis, where he makes lots of money working for a computer company. He drives over an hour and a half each way, and he works late every night. Sometimes he leaves the house at 5 a.m. and doesn't get home until after I'm in bed.

I trudge toward the house. Mom said she'd be back from work by the time I got home. "Mom?" I call, banging into the house. No answer. Before looking for her, I see the bag of "chore" clothes Mrs. Kyllo dropped off. She said every farm needs a stash of old clothes, and she wanted to make sure we had enough.

I pull out a faded Minnesota Vikings T-shirt and three maroon and gold ones from the University of Minnesota. There's also a Beckett's Feed Mill shirt, and one from King's Auto Supply Store, and three white ones with dark brown stains.

At the bottom is a T-shirt that must have once been white, but the back is streaked with blotches of pink. The front design—a girl in a pretty dress watering a huge flower garden—has totally been pinkified, so it's impossible to tell the original colors. "Bloom Where You're Planted" reads the message under the drawing in fat, fancy letters. It's the prettiest T-shirt in the bag, even if it is stained pink.

I pull on a pair of jeans too baggy for school, jam on my boots, and head outside. I peek into the chicken house. "Mom?" Butterscotch coos from a nest box, so I pet her. "Why can't all the hens be as nice as you?" She closes her eyes and leans into my touch. She is totally sweet, and I'm going to ask Mom never to make chicken soup out of Butterscotch.

Just then, I hear a familiar *peep, peep, peep*. I follow the sound to a barrel in front of the chicken house. Behind the barrel is my favorite duckling, a ball of yellow feathers with a little brown spot on the top of his head. I call him Lost and Found. The first time I saw him near the barn by himself, I scooped him up. "You're so lost," I said, "I'll help you get found." I tracked down Helen, the white duck, and put Lost and Found on the ground with the seven other ducklings. Since then, I've returned Lost and Found to his mama at least once a day. The little guy goes on too many adventures like his father, Mr. Duck, who's always waddling out into the sheep pasture.

Today I'm going to give Lost and Found a reason to stay close to home. I found an article online about how to make a little pond for ducklings, since they love to swim. Holding Lost and Found against my chest, I bang my way through the garage and pick up an old metal pan and two half-crumbled red bricks.

Mr. Duck, Helen, and the rest of the ducklings are hanging out in the shade under a pine tree. "Here you go, back to Mama." Lost and Found peeps and scoots over to Helen. About five feet from the ducks, I fill the pan with water. I put one brick in the pan and one on the ground next to it. The babies can use the bricks as steps until they're strong enough to jump in and out on their own.

Lost and Found is the first to investigate. He pecks at the brick, peeping softly, then hops up. He dips his beak into the water, climbs onto the edge of the pan, and plops in. In a few minutes the seven other ducklings join him. The last one does such a belly flop that the rest of the babies bob like rubber duckies in the bathtub. They paddle in circles, looking happy, while Helen cleans her feathers.

Mom will be amazed that I've done something farm-related without being asked. In a few minutes, I find her. She's sitting on a hay bale on the upper floor of the barn. She jumps when I climb the ladder, and even in the gloomy light, I see that her eyes are red rimmed and swollen, as if she's been crying. She's surrounded by bales jumbled up like toy blocks that have tipped over.

My duck pool forgotten, I point to the bales. "What happened?"

Mom slumps over. "I didn't stack them right. When I was almost done, I bumped against one of the bales and they all collapsed. Now I have to start all over."

In the past, Mom always asked me how my first day of school went. Not today.

"There must be a secret to stacking hay," I say.

Mom wipes her eyes and blows her nose. "My allergies are acting up," she says, not looking me in the eye. She's wearing a short-sleeved shirt, and her forearms are scratched and bloody.

"Want some help?"

Mom flashes me a tired look. "That'd be lovely." She shows me her arms. "But you'll need to wear long sleeves."

I begin backing toward the ladder. "Hey, Mom, after supper let's have a game night. How about Renaissance World or Aztec Challenge? Maybe Dad'll get home in time to play." We used to have a weekly game night when we lived in Minneapolis, but since moving to the farm, we've had exactly zero.

Mom wipes her face with a bandana. "I need to finish fencing that lower paddock."

"Sure, okay. Maybe another day."

On my way back to the house to change shirts, I pass the sheep standing near the barn. Most of them are afraid of me, so whenever I approach they leap straight into the air and scatter like dandelion seeds. It's kind of funny. The only two that don't run away are Ruby and Pearl. You can tell that Mrs. Sommers spoiled Ruby and Pearl because they are much fatter than the others. Ruby is reddish brown, with wool that looks like a faded rug. Pearl is pure white with a pretty face. Their eyes freak me out a little because their pupils are horizontal rectangles instead of round circles like people have.

Both stand waiting for me to scratch their wooly heads. I don't really love sheep, but these two are nice. They smell funny—Mom says it's the lanolin in their wool—but they follow me around a lot, so I've started touching them.

After I change into a long-sleeved shirt and return to the barn to help stack the bales, Mom touches my arm. "How was your first day?"

Her face is smudged with dirt. Her glasses are coated with hay dust. She doesn't want to hear that I wore sweaty barn boots to school and that Josh called me Boots all day. She doesn't want to hear about my first—and hopefully *only*—demerit.

"It went great," I say as I grab a bale and hoist it onto the top of the pile.

CHAPTER SIX

THIS MORNING I DECIDE TO COLLECT EGGS EARLY, WHEN the sun is barely peeking over the horizon. Mom and Dad have already left for work. Inside the chicken house, I reach into an empty box and find four smooth eggs. In the next box, there are seven. I decide I like this job, but then a hen cackles over my head and I jump. All the hens are up in the rafters! They haven't left for their day of pecking the ground and chasing after grasshoppers. Are they going to fly down and start pecking me again? Something plops onto the ground next to my foot. Fresh chicken poop. Erk! I flee the chicken house. No way am I staying in there if they're going to bomb me like that.

Today I'm ready when the bus arrives. I'm wearing the pink sandals I should have worn yesterday and jeans. I don't want any more Maybourne Sharpie notes in my student planner. I still haven't decided how to tell my parents about the demerit.

Caleigh is sitting with someone else, so I smile as I

walk past her and take an empty seat. The boys in the back yell, "Hey, Boots!" I turn around and make a face.

Once we get to school and I step off the bus, Josh brushes past me and mutters a few words. All I hear is "—something in your hair." Then he takes the steps two at a time and disappears inside. Something in my hair? I touch my bangs. I touch the sides of my head. My hair band is still holding everything back. I shake my head. Weirdo.

When I enter the Team Time room, Portia waves to me. I sit down in front of her and turn around. "You're amazing," she says. "You totally aced Maybourne yesterday!"

It's weird being a minor celebrity only because there were no sweatpants in the Lost and Found box.

Mr. Suarez clears his throat. "Okay, kids, let's get started." I turn to face him, and behind me Portia gasps.

"Taylor, don't move!" she cries. When I start twisting in my chair, Portia yelps. "Mr. Suarez, Taylor has something horrible in her hair."

I freeze.

"What?" the teacher asks.

"Something gross." I reach for the back of my head, but Portia grabs my wrist. "No, you don't want to touch it."

Mr. Suarez comes and stands beside me. "Taylor, I'm afraid you have a glop of what appears to be chicken . . . chicken . . ."

"Chicken poop?" I squeak.

"Don't move," he says. "I'll be right back."

The class groans. Someone a few rows over mutters, "I'm going to be sick."

I close my eyes. This is what Josh was trying to tell me.

Mr. Suarez returns with a paper towel and I feel a tug at the back of my head as he pulls off the chicken poop. The class groans again.

"I'll give you a pass so you can go clean your hair off with wet paper towels." As I stand up, he looks me in the eye, his face kind. "Some days don't go as well as other days, do they?"

I spend all of Team Time in the bathroom soaking the back of my head with wet towels, wiping and wiping and pulling and pulling until my scalp hurts. As I look at myself in the mirror, I imagine running away. I tried this when I was four. I packed a PB&J sandwich and a brownie, marched out the front door, and walked two blocks. I felt so tired I sat down on the curb and ate my lunch. I had to pee so I pulled down my pants and peed next to the curb. My parents came and got me. They love to tell the story at parties, which makes me blotch.

If I were to run away today, I'd take a bus back to Minneapolis and live with Lauren. I think about this as I return to class. The bell rings and I see Josh in the hallway, but he's fooling around with his friends and avoids me. I don't say anything because it might not be cool if his friends were to find out he actually tried to warn me about the poop in my hair.

I fantasize about running away until lunch. With my

tray loaded down with spaghetti, grapes, and a carton of milk, I survey the room. My heart sinks. The tables are full, but then a girl on the far side of the room stands and waves me over. Megan. I feel a little bounce in my step as I walk to her table. Girls smile as I walk by, still impressed that I got away with wearing a short skirt the entire first day of school.

"Taylor, this is Kelsey and Lisa."

I smile and say, "Hi."

"Megan said you live on a farm," Lisa says, her mouth full of salad.

I nod.

"Horses?"

"Sheep and goats."

Kelsey and Lisa moan. "I am *so* sorry for you," Kelsey says. "At least horses you can, you know, ride."

I listen to them talk about the riding stable they went to over the summer, and how Lisa fell off a horse. I laugh when they laugh, and it almost feels as if I'm starting to fit in.

"How do you like Melberg?" Megan asks.

I make a face. "It's kind of small."

Kelsey nods. "You were lucky to live in the Twin Cities. I bet you could go to the Mall of America whenever you wanted."

"I went there nearly every weekend."

They sigh. Megan takes the last bite of her apple. "Isn't it hard to go from living in a city to living on a farm outside of Melberg?"

"Yeah. My parents didn't ask what *I* wanted, they just bought the farm and dragged me down here."

Everyone groans. Then Megan says, "It must be a bummer to have your life totally change—school, house, friends, everything."

Something sticks in my throat and I nod. She gets it.

"The animals are okay, and I like collecting the eggs, and we have this really cute little duckling I named Lost and Found, but my parents are always busy working and fixing fences and repairing the barn. I never see them. And they've become total klutzes. They need a bumper sticker that says 'Farming can be dangerous to your health.'"

Lisa laughs, then stops, her gaze on Megan. "What?"

"Nothing."

"Oh, no. I recognize that look. You're thinking about something." Lisa turns to me. "Megan gets these big ideas, and they usually end up getting one of us in trouble."

Megan does look as if she has a secret to tell. Her cheeks are flushed, like she's been running. "I'm thinking, that's all."

The other girls laugh as we stand up with our trays. "We're in trouble now," Kelsey says, more amused than worried.

Megan shoots me a look and goose bumps pop up on my arms. Clearly her idea, whatever it is, has something to do with me. Maybe she can help me bloom where I've been planted, just like it says on the T-shirt.

CHAPTER SEVEN

THURSDAY NIGHT I ACTUALLY SEE DAD. WE MEET IN THE hallway. He tips his head. "You look vaguely familiar."

"I used to have a dad who looks like you," I say. Then he growls and scoops me up in a hug. I squeeze him around the neck, and he puts me down. I touch the Band-Aid on his forearm. "What happened to you?"

"Gouged myself on a rusty nail in the barn. Stings like crazy."

Mom yells from the kitchen. "Don't forget to get a tetanus shot tomorrow. The receptionist said you don't need an appointment."

I tip my head. "Tetanus?"

Dad grins. "It's a disease that enters your body through a cut or scrape. It attacks your muscles, and..." His shoulder jerks suddenly and one arm cramps against his chest. Alarm pulses through me. His other arm jerks into a weird position. "Until you're so locked up—" Now he makes a horrible face and freezes that way.

I stare at him, wondering how long he can hold this

ridiculous pose. His eyes are twinkling. "That is *so* not funny," I finally say.

He relaxes his arms and face. "Really? Because I thought it was kind of funny."

I roll my eyes and push him playfully toward the kitchen. "Tomorrow's Friday, Dad. Can you stay home? You could get a tetanus shot in Melberg."

"No can do, kiddo. Early meeting with new client."

"Erk," I say.

Dad laughs. "Double Erk. But what if I reserve Saturday for Taylor Time?"

"Finally," I say. "Wii bowling?"

"Yup."

"And the Mall of America? Mom says I need new shoes."

"Sounds good. How's school, by the way?"

"It's okay. We have these student planners that we have to carry with us all the time, and that's kind of lame."

"It probably teaches you organizational skills, responsibility, stuff like that."

Mom's sitting at the table, looking tired. "Michael, did I hear you say you have an early meeting tomorrow?"

Something passes between my parents. Neither says a word, but I can tell they're talking with their eyes. Mom sighs and turns to me. "I have tomorrow off so I'm taking Jersey to the vet first thing in the morning. He needs a check up, and it's cheaper to take him in instead of asking the vet to come here. I need a favor. Could you close the pen gate and the barn door behind me after I lead Jersey out? I'll take you to school on my way to the vet."

I grab an apple from the bowl on the counter. "That's it? Just open and close the gate?"

"Yup."

I shrug. "I can do that."

Early Friday morning, I find an umbrella in the front closet. When I enter the chicken house, I open the umbrella and a few hens up in the rafters cluck in alarm. As I collect eggs, I feel something plop onto the umbrella. "Ha, missed me," I say. When I go back outside, I spray down the poor, traumatized umbrella with the hose by the front porch.

After I collect eggs, I drop my backpack and sandals in Mom's truck so I won't forget to change out of my boots. Mom and I head for the barn.

While Mom backs the truck up to the barn door, I reach into the sheep pen and rub Ruby's side. She grunts and leans closer, so I scratch harder. Pearl comes running when she hears Ruby's grunts. *Hey, no fair. Scratch me too!*

I stop and help Mom wheel the loading ramp up to the back of the pickup. "Why are Ruby and Pearl fatter than the other sheep?"

"Good eaters, I guess." Mom finishes setting up the ramp. "Let's get Jersey."

As we near the goat pen, I plug my nose. Jersey, an

all-white goat, stands in the pen nuzzling one of the three brown female goats. Then he steps back, and—whoa!—he lowers his head between his front legs and pees on it.

"Mom! He's peeing on himself!" With his front leg, Jersey rubs the pee all over his head until his white hair's stained a dirty yellow.

"I think I'm going to be sick," I say.

Mom laughs. "He's making himself attractive to the ladies."

"Gross."

"I'll put the halter on Jersey and lead him from the pen. You make sure the other goats don't follow us out, okay?"

Jersey tosses his head a few times, but Mom's able to get the halter on him. After Mom leads him out, I close the gate, then close the barn door behind us. Easy.

When Jersey is free of the barn, however, he begins pulling on his rope. "Jersey, here," Mom says. "Up the ramp like a good boy."

But Jersey isn't a good boy. My mouth drops open as Jersey begins pulling Mom around the gravel driveway. "Whoa, whoa!" Mom yells. Jersey changes direction and Mom falls to her knees, but she doesn't let go.

I run to cut Jersey off. "Whoa!" I yell. Jersey stops and Mom crawls to her feet, yanking on the rope and throwing her arms around the goat's neck. She tries steering him toward the ramp, but he whirls in circles and the rope wraps around Mom's feet. "Whoa!" she yells. "Jersey, stop!"

I dance beside them as Jersey drags Mom farther from the truck. Then he jerks his head into Mom's face, and she cries out. Blood gushes from her nose.

"Mom! Let go!"

"No, I'll never catch him again." Blood smears her face, her shirt, and Jersey's shoulder.

I fling my arms around Jersey's chest, nearly knocking him over. Startled, he stops fighting, and Mom and I half-walk, half-drag him to the ramp and push him up into the pickup. Mom shoves the ramp out of the way, slams the tailgate shut, lowers the topper door, and collapses onto the ramp, blood everywhere.

Hands shaking, I pull Mom's bandana off her head and press it against her bloody nose. "Mom, are you okay?"

She nods, eyes closed, breath ragged. "Jersey might have broken my nose."

My hands are grimy from Jersey's hair, and bits of straw cling to my clothes. "I need to clean up."

"No time," Mom whispers. "We have to go."

Mom starts the truck, her hands trembling as they grasp the wheel. I lower the windows for some fresh air in case Mom feels faint. The smell of cow manure from a nearby farm blasts through the windows. The breeze feels good even though it stinks. Our hair whips around our faces as the truck whizzes down the road. There isn't a peep from Jersey. I take off my boots, dusty from the scuffle, and put on my sandals.

"You need to see a doctor," I shout over the wind and

road noise as I pick straw off my jeans.

Mom nods. "I will."

As we ride, I feel angry, but I don't know if I'm angry at Jersey or at Mom. She's probably never tried to lead a goat anywhere, but she acts as if she knows what she's doing. Bits of blood are smeared across her cheek and in the crease of her nose. She pulls up to the school and manages a smile. "Never a dull moment, eh? How many girls get to dance with a goat before school?" Her hair's tangled but she's grinning. "Now don't worry. I'll go to the emergency room to see about my nose. Oh, and let's don't tell Dad about this, okay?"

"Okay." I slide from the truck and sprint up the school steps. I dash into the nearest restroom to wash my hands, race down the hall with three other nearly tardy students, and slip into Team Time just before the bell.

The girl sitting ahead of me whirls around. "What's that smell? You totally *reek.*"

"Me?"

Other kids begin moaning and plugging their noses. Someone behind me gags.

"Smells like something died."

"Smells like pee."

"Stinks like garbage."

I sniff my hands. I sniff my sleeve. "I don't smell anything."

"You wouldn't," snaps the boy next to me. "Your nose

is too full of stink."

"Let's settle down," Mr. Suarez says. "Time for school announcements."

"Mr. Suarez, Boots stinks. I'm going to die," says a girl who's not even sitting near me.

"Sonya, I doubt you will expire from the smell." Mr. Suarez gives me a friendly grin. "Taylor, another farming adventure?"

I'm so horrified my throat closes up. "A goat," is all I can choke out. For a second I close my eyes. Please, let an earthquake come and swallow me. Please, let a tsunami hit the school and drown me. Please, let a big scary meteor end all life on earth.

I open my eyes. Nothing like that has happened. I'm still in school. Still alive. Still reeking of goat. And more miserable than I've ever been in my whole life.

CHAPTER EIGHT

I WASH MY HANDS AGAIN AFTER TEAM TIME, BUT IT DOES NO good. Jersey is in my hair and on my clothes and I'm going to smell this way for the rest of my life. In English class, Ms. Benton has a cold so she can't smell anything and scolds the class for making such a "fuss." She assigns *The Magician's Elephant,* which I read last year, and hands out copies of the book. Then Mr. Maybourne comes to the door and while he and Ms. Benton whisper about something, kids pinch their noses and say "Pe-uw." Someone snorts like a pig. I pretend to be reading my book, praying Mr. Maybourne can't smell me. There's probably a regulation in the handbook about coming to school smelling like a goat.

In math class, Josh walks in, then starts sniffing. "Something stinks around here!" He looks at me and laughs. "Hey, it's Boots!" Everyone wrinkles up their noses.

By the end of math class, I'm a wreck. When the bell rings, I run to the bathroom on the second floor and lock myself in the last stall. The bell for next period rings and I lean against the stall door and hug myself. I'm not going to budge. Out in the hall, a teacher stops someone without a pass, but the voices and footsteps quickly fade. I fight back tears. I fantasize that tonight Mom and Dad will sit me down and explain that I'm old enough to know the truth. I'm adopted, they'll say. Then a man and woman will come to the house and introduce themselves as my birth parents. "Would you like to come live with us now? We can give you a great life."

"Do you have goats?" I'll ask. They'll shake their heads. "Any barn boots? Chicken poop?" They'll shake their heads again and I'll pack a bag and leave Mom and Dad and the farm.

The fantasy makes me feel sick to my stomach. If I ever left the farm, I'd want my parents to come with me.

After a while the bell rings and the hall explodes with noise. Girls bang into the bathroom.

"Pe-uw," one girl says. "What's that smell?"

"Duh. We're in the bathroom."

"My grandma once had a dead mouse under her sofa. It smelled like this."

Girls complain and cough and flush toilets and shriek at bad hair. Then they take their noise with them, leaving only silence. A minute later, the door opens again and a single pair of feet enter.

"Rumor has it that the second floor girls' bathroom smells like something died." It's Megan.

I moan. "Don't come any closer. The smell will kill you."

Megan's laugh is like a warm hug, and suddenly I don't feel so alone. She stops at my stall, drops to her knees, and peers under the door. "Hi."

"Hi."

"Need some help?"

"No, I like smelling this way."

"Didn't anyone tell you the nurse has a big sink and some shampoo and soap? And that she has a secret stash of clothing for any student who throws up or something?"

I sigh. "No, they didn't."

Megan escorts me to the nurse's office, gets a hall pass from the nurse, and with a friendly wave, leaves to return to class.

Nurse Winston is short and wide and brisk. "First, out of those clothes." Soon I'm dressed in a pair of gray sweatpants so baggy the nurse has to tighten them with a purple belt. After I shrug on a pink Little Mermaid sweatshirt, I can barely stand to look at myself.

Next the nurse washes my hair in the sink and gives me a blow dryer. "Twenty years from now this will be a funny memory."

I dry my hair, irritated. Adults always say that, and it's stupid. Who *cares* about twenty years from now?

When I shut off the dryer, I turn on my cell and it beeps with a message. "Tay, it's Mom. Call me. I'm having an interesting day, so I imagine you are too. Funny how many people dislike the smell of goat." I snort.

The bell rings for the next class, so I head for the girls' bathroom again and call Mom.

"Hey, kiddo," she says. "How's your day been?"

"I'm wearing sweatpants that are three sizes too big and a Little Mermaid sweatshirt."

"Ouch. You hated that movie." Pause. "Maybe you feel so sick you need to leave school?"

"You think?"

"I'll be there in fifteen minutes. Meet me out front. I have a surprise for you."

She hangs up.

CHAPTER NINE

I WAIT FOR MOM IN THE SCHOOL'S OFFICE AS RAIN SPLATters against the windows. Mom called the office and told them she'd be picking me up because I feel sick, and that's totally true.

When I see the rusty red pickup through the window, I run outside. Mom gives me a sad smile, or maybe she looks sad because of the narrow white bandage stretched across her nose. "Be right back." She runs into the office to sign me out while I sit in the truck. I watch rivulets of rain stream down the windshield and dream again about being adopted.

"Done. You're legally excused. You smell good," Mom says as she climbs into the truck.

"So do you. What's the surprise?"

Mom's smile is brighter now. "I'm having a spinning lesson today, and now you get to have one too."

"A spinning lesson? Mom, this is the twenty-first century. They have machines that do that kind of thing."

"Ah, but it's not the same. I remember going to the State Fair when I was a kid and standing in the Sheep Barn watching this woman spin. First she sheared fleece off the sheep that was standing right beside her. She sort of fluffed it up and then spun it into yarn on this big old wheel. It was magic, and I couldn't stop watching."

Mom turns down the street that leads to the tallest building in town, ten stories of housing for senior citizens. She pulls up in front of the high rise. "Here we are. You're in for a treat, Tay. You're about to meet Mrs. Florence Sommers."

"The lady who sold you the farm?"

"The very one. She knows how to spin and dye and knit and weave, and that's one of the reasons she raised sheep for so many years." Mom pulls a new spinning wheel made of blond wood from the back of the pickup. "Let's go."

We ride the elevator, which smells like lavender, to the tenth floor. It opens into a wide hallway with blue and burgundy carpeting that looks like leaves scattered down a sidewalk. Mom rings the buzzer.

Mrs. Florence Sommers is tall and straight, with long gray hair pulled back into a thick braid. She wears a red blouse, tan slacks, and a hot pink cardigan sweater. Her face is as white as the paint on her apartment door, but when she shakes my hand, I see that her eyes are a faded blue, like denim that's gone through the laundry a hundred times. Across the backs of her hands, veins twist like ropes.

"Welcome, welcome!" She pulls me through the door with amazing strength, probably because she has wrestled sheep most of her life. "Two for today's lesson. How lovely."

The apartment is neat and clean and isn't old-lady-ish at all. Bright flower prints splash across one wall, and the light blue sofa looks soft as a pillow. But the best part of the apartment is the TV in the corner of the living room. After politely accepting a glass of water and a cookie, I drift toward it. A soap opera is playing. Do I dare change the channel? Does Mrs. Sommers have cable? Could I watch a rerun of Celebrity Star Stage?

Mrs. Sommers opens a canvas bag and pulls out a long rope of white fuzzy stuff. "Here's the last of Pearl's fleece." She teaches Mom the parts of the wheel—spindle, treadle, bobbin, and a few other words I can't catch. It's so amazing to be watching TV that I don't care that soap operas aren't my thing. Even the commercials are fun to watch.

"This rope of fleece is called roving, and that's what you spin into yarn. First, attach the end of the roving to this bit of yarn already coming through the black hole there. Wool has little barbs on it that help it stick together. Start the wheel spinning with your hand, use your foot on the treadle to keep it spinning, and feed the roving into the black hole, which I call the thingamabob. You want the roving at that point to be very thin, so you draw it out with your other hand."

Mom repeats the instructions, then uses her hand to

send the wheel spinning. "Oh, shoot! It broke." It takes Mrs. Sommers ten minutes to teach Mom how to start the wheel spinning without breaking the thread going into the thingamabob.

"Oh, shoot." Mom starts again. "Shoot."

"That's all right," Mrs. Sommers says. "Be patient. It's a matter of finding the right touch, spinning the wheel fast enough to draw in the fiber, but not so fast that it breaks."

"Oh, shoot."

I bite back a giggle. Knowing Mom, in a few minutes her "shoots" are going to turn into something less polite. Her face is red, her brow tight with concentration.

"Look, I'm doing it! I'm doing it! Finally . . . . Oh, shoot."

Mrs. Sommers winks at me. "Taylor, would you like to try? Your mom needs a break."

Mom shakes out her hands and stretches them toward the ceiling. "C'mon, honey, it's fun."

"It didn't sound very fun," I say as I stand.

Mom grimaces. "Florence, I need to use your bathroom. Then I'll freshen up our coffee."

I sit on the chair in front of the wheel and Mrs. Sommers puts a pile of fluffy stuff in my lap. "See how wool wants to stick together?" She stretches it out to show me how the fibers cling to each other. "That's why spinning works."

She walks me through the same steps she did with Mom and helps me start the wheel. The roving feels like cotton candy in my hands.

"That's it. Stretch it out thinner. Keep treadling. Move your hands here. What a light touch you have!" I watch as the filmy roving disappears into the thingamabob and comes out the other side as yarn winding around a bobbin. "Excellent, Taylor. You have natural aptitude."

My foot pumps the treadle and I keep spinning, but suddenly I feel awkward. What should I say next? What do you say to someone old?

"Nice apartment, Mrs. Sommers," I say as I focus on the roving slipping through my fingers. The yarn coming out the other side is going from fat to thin to fat, which can't be right, but Mrs. Sommers doesn't stop me.

"Call me Florence." She watches me for a while. "Did you know that three hundred years ago, children had to spend hours each day spinning?"

I accidentally drop the roving and it flips around and around and jams itself into the thingamabob. "Erk!"

Chuckling, Florence shows me how to unsnarl the mess and start up again.

"Everyone had to help," she says. "In order to sew clothing, people needed fabric. To weave fabric, they needed yarn. The only way to get yarn was to spin it."

"How long does it take to spin enough yarn to make a sweater?" I'm getting the hang of it, so the yarn starts coming out the same size.

"You don't want to know," Florence says.

"Thank goodness they invented the Mall of America."

Florence laughs.

I begin spinning again. "Mrs. Sommers, have—"

"Florence."

"Okay, Florence, have you ever watched Celebrity Star Stage?"

"It's my favorite show."

I grin so widely that my cheeks hurt.

"Haven't your parents gotten you a satellite dish yet? Mine broke in a storm just before I sold the place."

I make a sad face and she laughs again. "If I record a few shows, will you come back and spin some more?"

As I nod, Mom comes out of the kitchen and stands behind me. "Wow. Look at you go." She sounds proud and envious at the same time. I'm sorry I'm better at this than she is, but she *did* send me to school smelling like a goat, so it seems only fair.

CHAPTER TEN

SATURDAY MORNING MOM HAS TO WORK, AND DAD STAYS home like he said he would. We plan our day: caramel apple pancakes, farm chores, the Wii bowling tournament, the trip to the Mall of America for shoes.

The pancakes are nummy. Dad helps me collect eggs, and he laughs at my umbrella. But when we're done, there are two blobs of poop on my umbrella and two on Dad's shoulders.

As we pass the ducks, Lost and Found isn't with the others. Dad and I look for him behind the chicken house and I hear his soft peeping. "There you are." I scoop him up and deposit him in front of Helen. "What a bad mama you are. Can't keep track of all your babies." Then I help Dad feed the goats.

During the bowling tournament, Dad keeps trying to put weird spins on the ball, and ends up knocking down exactly zero pins. I know he's paying more attention to making me laugh than to winning the game. This is good Dad behavior. Of course, I totally beat him.

As we get ready to leave for Minneapolis, I hear the goats bleating. They sound like people in a burning building yelling "Fire! Fire!" I decide to ignore them, but as we get into the car, the goats bleat even louder.

"That's not normal, is it?" Dad asks.

I shake my head. "Mom says the goats only bleat if they're hungry or upset. We've already fed them."

Sighing, Dad signals us back to the house. We yank on our barn boots and head for the goats. They're in their pen outside the barn. All five are looking off into the distance. "What's wrong with them?" Dad asks.

"I don't have a clue." The goats are dancing back and forth along the fence. They clearly want to go somewhere. Then it hits me. The sheep are supposed to be in the pasture that slopes down from the barn. The goats like watching the sheep. "Dad, where are the sheep?"

We run to the edge of the sheep pasture and scan for the flock. How can twenty sheep just disappear? Dad figures it out. He points to a red gate in the distance, swinging back and forth in the breeze. He says bad words that I won't repeat. "I was supposed to fix that gate. The latch was loose." He clutches his head. "This is bad. This is very bad. The sheep must be in the neighbor's alfalfa field."

We start running through the pasture. I try not to think about the fact that I might be stepping in sheep poop, but Dad is running too fast for me to watch the ground. "Why is this bad?" I ask as I try to keep up.

"Your mom explained this to me the other night.

Sheep love alfalfa, but because they haven't been eating it, their stomachs can't digest it right now." He pants as we climb over a fallen tree stretching across the ground. "They need to start eating alfalfa slowly to give their stomachs time to adjust. If they eat too much too fast, they might bloat up and die." We're both gasping as we reach the open gate. I don't understand bloat, but I get the die part.

We run through the knee-high alfalfa, which is harder than you'd think. "Mom will kill us if her sheep die on our day to watch them," I say. It's hard to run because there are big clumps of dirt under the alfalfa plants. Dad and I both fall twice. Finally we reach the top of a small slope and see the sheep. They are happily munching on the green stuff that is going to kill them.

We bend over, struggling to breathe. "Okay, okay," Dad finally says. "We need to get them back through the gate."

"When the sheep are at the bottom of the hill, Mom calls them and they come," I offer.

Dad wipes his forehead with his T-shirt sleeve. "Worth a try."

I clap my hands like Mom. "Here, sheepies. Here, sheepies." I feel stupid. It sounds like I'm calling a dog.

The sheep all raise their heads, but they don't come. They keep gobbling mouthfuls of alfalfa. Dad swears again. He's thinking bloat. He's thinking dead sheep. "Okay," Dad says. "You circle around behind them to the right and I'll go to the left. We'll herd them back toward the gate."

After Dad and I meet behind the flock, the sheep miraculously start moving forward toward the gate. It's going to work. But as we come up closer, the sheep suddenly turn to face us. We wave our arms and keep walking. A few sheep bleat and look frightened. I see Ruby and Pearl in the crowd, but they don't come when I call. Then all the sheep start running—straight toward us! We wave our arms and shout, but they run right past us.

For twenty minutes Dad and I run and chase and yell. My knees hurt from falling down, and Dad's voice is hoarse from yelling. But at least the sheep are so busy running they're not eating the deadly alfalfa. We can't get them anywhere near the gate.

Dad's face is red and neither of us is laughing anymore. We stop again and try to breathe. "This isn't working," Dad says. "We need a herding dog."

"You think?" I raise my hand in apology before Dad can scold me. He thinks sarcasm is unattractive in a twelve-year-old.

"What do sheep like to eat more than alfalfa?" Dad asks.

I snap my fingers. "Corn. They love corn. Ruby and Pearl are always begging for it."

Dad looks back toward our barn, then slumps over. "I thought I was in better shape than this."

I'm tired too, but I am younger. "I'll go, Dad." I trudge through the alfalfa, through the gate, and up the hill to the barn. The goats are still standing there, bleating. I find a small bucket and fill it with corn, then trudge-trudge-trudge back to Dad. "I've seen Mom do this," I say. I lift the bucket up and rattle the corn. "Here, sheepies. Here, sheepies."

Ruby and Pearl look up. I shake the bucket again. "It's working," Dad says. More sheep raise their heads. "Okay, here's the plan. You keep rattling the bucket and walk slowly back, leading them through the gate. I'll walk behind them to chase stragglers and then I'll *tie* that gate shut."

He circles the flock as I keep rattling. Now all the sheep are watching me. Ruby finally starts toward me. "C'mon, Ruby," I call. "Sheep candy!" Ruby begins to run, and the rest of the sheep follow. Yes!

No! What if they reach me before I reach the gate? I turn and run through the alfalfa. My boots are so heavy I can barely lift them. Behind me eighty little sheep hooves go swish-swish through the plants. I glance over my shoulder. They're almost on top of me.

"Run faster," Dad yells from somewhere behind me. I pour it on and start leaping over the alfalfa instead of trudging through it. I'm nearly to the gate. I can hear the sheep grunting because they are right on my heels. If I fall now, they'll trample me. I clutch the bucket to my chest and run for my life.

The sheep move up beside me and we all run through the gate. My lungs are on fire and my legs weigh one hundred pounds each, but I don't dare stop running. Yet when I reach the fallen tree, I can't go any farther. I slow down, but luckily, so do the sheep. I finally stop, my lungs burning as the sheep gather around me. They want that corn! They reach long noses toward the bucket. I lift it over my head but that only makes them start jumping. They push and shove against me until my body gets twisted one way and my feet get twisted another. Dad yells something from the gate. A sheep jumps up on me. The bucket flies out of my hands and I go down.

"Taylor!"

I curl up in a ball as the sheep fight over the spilled corn. They bump me and nose my clothes as they gobble up the corn. When I realize they aren't going to kill me, the whole thing is kind of funny.

"Outta the way! Move!" Dad yells, then trips and falls hard on the ground next to me with a cry of pain. He flings a protective arm over me. "Are you okay?"

Dad's arrival scares the sheep, and they move a few feet away. I roll onto my back, amazed I've survived. "Yeah, I'm fine. What happened to you just now?"

Dad grimaces and reaches for his ankle. "Twisted it when I fell."

We lay on our backs in the grass, staring at the blue sky. That's all we can see because we're surrounded by a ring of wool. The sheep are determined to find every kernel of corn I spilled. They snort as they search through the grass.

"Well," Dad finally says. "I've enjoyed the quality time we've spent together today, haven't you?"

I grin. "It's been very special." I roll on my side to face him. "Shouldn't you put some ice on your ankle?"

"I suppose. Shouldn't you get that fresh sheep poop off your jeans?"

I shriek. Pieces of squashed Milk Dud-like poop cling to my hip and leg. I shriek again. We climb to our feet, and Dad brushes off the poop. We laugh so hard that I actually start crying a little.

After I help Dad limp back to the house, he squeezes my shoulder. "Let's don't tell your mother about this, okay?"

"About the ankle?"

"About the open gate and the sheep in the alfalfa. She might get upset."

"What if they bloat up and die?"

He lies down on the couch with an ice pack on his ankle. "If you could check on them this afternoon, that would be great. If they're wool-covered balloons, then they're bloating and we'd better call the vet."

I put a frozen pizza in the oven. After we eat, Dad takes some aspirin and falls asleep. There's no way I'm getting to the Mall today. I walk outside and check the sheep. Other than Ruby and Pearl, none of the sheep look like balloons.

I finally sit down and read the student handbook from beginning to end. It has categories like "Bus Expectations" and "Behavior Consequences" and "False Fire Alarms." The Clothing section is the weirdest. Some of it makes sense, like "no clothing or jewelry with designs that promote prejudice or unlawful acts." And items that could be "used as weapons" are prohibited.

But the skirts? One inch below the fingertips? I make a light line on my leg with magic marker. Unbelievable. But I will follow the rules because that's the kind of person I am. And I don't want any more embarrassing moments with Mr. Maybourne. I finish reading the handbook and stick it in a folder.

I can't watch a DVD because Dad's asleep in front of the TV. I check the sheep again and they all look fine. I agree with Dad. No need to tell Mom that the sheep were bad. She has enough to think about without worrying about the sheep bloating up and dying.

Time to do some homework. When I open my planner to check the assignment, there it is: Maybourne's comment in harsh felt tip: *Skirt alarmingly short.* Should I show my parents? Mom is tired from working at the grain elevator and on the farm. Dad has a sore ankle. I slip into the office where Mom pays bills and find her signature on a letter. I study it, then copy it a few times. Easy. I find a black felt tip—if you're going to forge a signature, be bold. I sign on the line, *Kirsten McNamara.*

I stare at what I've done. It's for the best. Really.

Then I sit down at Mom's spinning wheel in the living room and start spinning. The wheel's so quiet Dad doesn't wake up. I spin and spin and spin.

CHAPTER ELEVEN

THE SWELLING IN DAD'S ANKLE GOES DOWN, AND HE'S not limping when Mom comes home. "Anything exciting happen while I was gone?" Mom asks.

I give Dad a panicked look.

"Taylor beat me in bowling again," Dad says.

It feels weird not to tell Mom everything. How can living on a farm be a good thing if we have to hide stuff from one another?

The next afternoon Mom and I drive to Florence's for another spinning lesson. Florence greets us in lime green slacks and a Hawaiian shirt. She nods toward the TV. "Celebrity Star Stage, rerun on Channel 103."

I yelp and fling myself onto the blue sofa, while Mom sets up her wheel. She examines her bobbins. "Wow, I don't remember spinning this much." She gives me a funny look.

"It looks lovely, Kirsten. Very uniform."

I'm so happy about the TV that I lose myself in an hour of singing and dancing and celebrity judges. Now I can talk with Megan about Kyle Morris's weird hair and Brittany Berkshire's awesome voice.

When the show ends, I hear low voices coming from the kitchen. I turn the volume down. I don't know why, but I love hearing stuff that isn't meant for my ears.

Mom's voice has an edge to it. "It's hard, Florence. It's so much harder than I expected."

"It's partly my fault. I shouldn't have sold you the animals. You had to jump in too deep, too fast."

I lift myself off the sofa and sneak closer, staying near the wall.

"Look at my arms. They're covered with scabs because I keep scraping myself on the edges of cattle panel or on fence posts. Michael gouged his arm on a rusty nail. And I think he fell yesterday but he's too embarrassed to tell me."

"You need to slow down. Farmers have accidents all the time, especially if they're beginners. You're using tools and equipment that are unfamiliar. You don't know the ground yet. You'll get the hang of it. Here, look."

I peek around the corner to see Florence rolling up her sleeve. "Feel the scars on my arm."

"Goodness," Mom says. "Scars are just the beginning, though. One of the chickens died this morning."

Mom had found a brown hen in the yard with its head bitten off. She suspected a weasel did it. I was sorry the poor hen died, but I was relieved it wasn't Butterscotch.

After Mom threw the dead chicken into the dumpster, I tried asking her about it, but she shook her head and waved me away, as if she were about to cry.

"Oh, dearie, you have forty chickens of all ages—"

"Thirty-nine now."

"Don't worry. Chickens are going to die of unseen illnesses or old age. A fox or a hawk or an eagle might swoop down and take one. A car might run over another. Stuff happens, especially when you're caring for sixty-five animals."

"Seventy-three. Helen and Mr. Duck have eight ducklings."

"Oh, how I miss the ducklings. But remember, with that many animals, some are bound to die. It's a normal part of farm life." Her words make sense, but after hearing the list of how chickens can die, I worry about Butterscotch.

"Ever since I was a kid, I wanted to live on a farm," Mom says. "I wanted sheep and goats and chickens. I wanted to sit in my charming farmhouse and spin my own yarn and knit socks. But nothing feels quite right. It's like I'm a stranger in my own life."

Florence says something too low for me to catch.

"I know, but Michael's exhausted from commuting every day. He tries to help when he gets home, but he's so tired. Taylor tries too, but now that school's started, she needs to focus on her homework."

"And you need to be less of a perfectionist," Florence

says. "You've totally changed your way of life. You need to give yourself more time to adjust."

"I guess." Mom's long sigh makes me sad. "I'm sorry, I shouldn't be complaining to you. I'm delighted that we bought your house and that we're on your farm, but I wish I knew more. Take Pearl and Ruby. They are so much fatter than the other sheep, but I'm not feeding them much corn, so it can't be that."

"When you say fatter, what do you mean?"

"Wider, like they've each swallowed a box or something."

"Oh, dear, oh dear." My ears perk up. I grab the remote and reduce the volume. "Let me see. It's early September. Going back five months puts us at May. Oh, dear, oh, dear."

"What?"

"Mid-May, two days before I sold my ram Erik, I found him in with a few of the sheep. I didn't think he'd mated with any of them because it was the wrong time of year. But he might have bred Ruby and Pearl, because from the sound of things, they could be pregnant."

"Pregnant?" Mom doesn't sound happy.

"You should have the vet ultrasound both sheep to find out. If my calculations are correct, those two sheep are not only pregnant, they are *very* pregnant. They could give birth any day now. Watch each ewe's udder. When it fills up with milk and becomes so tight that it shines, the ewe's about to give birth."

"Baby lambs. Oh my. I wasn't planning on babies so soon."

I sneak back to the sofa and sit down. Lambs might be fun. I could cuddle them and maybe give them names. But Mom doesn't sound excited at all.

CHAPTER TWELVE

MONDAY MORNING I WAKE UP SO EARLY IT'S STILL DARK outside. After last week, I'm not looking forward to school. What will go wrong this week? It's as if I've swallowed a Doom and Gloom pill. I want to wear a skirt, so I measure each one against the denim skirt and find a pink one that's two inches longer. This should keep me off Maybourne's radar. Unfortunately the top I pick is so short that one inch of my midriff shows, which is illegal according to the student handbook. I change tops and add a sweater. After breakfast, when the sun is struggling to climb higher in the pale morning sky and Mom and Dad have left for work, I go outside to do chores.

No hens peck me when I gather the eggs. No one poops on my umbrella. Butterscotch is sweet. And I set a record for the number of eggs collected in one morning—twenty-four! When I leave the chicken house, all the chickens are outside pecking at the ground. Helen and her eight babies walk by. Lost and Found is actually with them. But as they pass, the ducklings cross some invisible line into Chicken Territory. A black hen squawks and grabs the nearest duckling by the neck. It's Lost and Found! She shakes him back and forth, he peeps in protest, and Helen starts hissing. I run toward the black hen, waving my arms and yelling, and she drops Lost and Found. I pick him up. He's panting but he's okay.

Then Helen charges me, wings flapping, mouth open. She leaps up and bites me on the knee. The pudgy part. I yell and step back, but she doesn't let go. She's hanging off my knee and it really hurts. "Off! Off!" I shriek and then place Lost and Found on the ground. When I do Helen lets go, nudges Lost and Found with her wicked beak, and stalks off. The babies waddle behind her.

I stand there, stunned. I've never been attacked by a duck before. Has anyone? I've never heard of such a thing. But then I'd never heard of wearing chicken poop to school or reeking like a goat, either. Sighing, I walk back to the house. I slip into my sandals and begin my lonely wait for the bus. In Minneapolis ten of us took the same bus. Sometimes all the noise got to me, but today I miss it.

During Team Time, Mr. Suarez walks by each desk to check student planners. He opens my book and sees my one demerit with the forged signature next to it. He initials my book, so my *Kirsten McNamara* forgery passes, but as he hands back my planner, he looks down at my legs. "Another farming adventure?"

"What?"

"Your knee is bleeding," he says.

Oh, no. There's dried blood around two little puncture marks on my left knee. I moan and gently bang my forehead against the desk. Everyone laughs.

Mr. Suarez chuckles. "Okay, inquiring minds want to know. What happened?"

I blotch. "I was attacked by a duck." The whole class roars and then I start laughing too. It is sort of funny. "I had no idea ducks could do such a thing," I say, standing up and accepting a hall pass from Mr. Suarez.

Nurse Winston cleans my knee and takes a Band-Aid from a box.

"Don't you have any others?" I ask.

"No, sorry." I return to Team Time wearing a black and yellow Band-Aid that says "Crime Scene—Do Not Cross."

In Social Studies, Mrs. Walker announces we're having special visitors. Four kids in navy blue jackets covered in badges and pins file in. "Members of our local 4-H are here to explain the organization and give examples of 4-H projects."

4-H kids had actually come to my school in Minneapolis, too, and at lunch Lauren and I had made fun of their jackets and little badges. In a rare flash of wit, I'd asked the girls at our table, "Hey, you know what 4-H stands for? Ho-hum, ho-hum."

One kid entering the Melberg classroom carries a

black rabbit, another holds a red chicken with wild fuzzy feathers on its head. A third carries a poster about the dangers of oil spills, and the fourth is Caleigh holding a knit sweater.

"Every year," begins Mrs. Walker, "we encourage students to get involved in 4-H. It's a great way for city students to interact with animals, and for those kids living on farms to gain more knowledge and experience."

The kids explain their projects. Caleigh knit her sweater herself, and it's really cute, mostly sky blue with black and white cows walking along above the hem. I'm not big on farming, but cows on clothing crack me up. Maybe Caleigh would knit something out of the yarn I'm spinning. Wait. Who am I kidding? It would take me ten years to spin enough yarn for a sweater.

When the kids are done, Mrs. Walker scans the room. "Taylor, you're from the Twin Cities, so 4-H might be unfamiliar to you. Would you like to guess what 4-H stands for?"

Upon hearing my name, a few kids nearby wave hands in front of their noses as if I still smell. I don't know what comes over me. I should shrug and say, "I don't know." I should say, "Home? Health?" and let someone else finish. But instead, I open my Minneapolis mouth and say, "Ho-hum, ho-hum."

Absolute silence. You could have heard an eraser drop. Caleigh turns bright red.

"I'm just kidding," I say lamely. "I don't really know.

I'm sure it's totally interesting. I don't . . . "

Caleigh finds her voice. "Head, heart, hands, health."

Mrs. Walker glares at me, then turns to the 4-H kids. "Thank you, Caleigh. It's a wonderful program."

That afternoon Caleigh walks right past me on the bus and sits with someone else.

I can't blame her, so I sit by myself and stare out the window. I wonder if a discombobulated person can "bloom" like it says on my chore T-shirt. Judging from my Melberg life so far, maybe not.

CHAPTER THIRTEEN

MEGAN ARRIVES IN THE CAFETERIA OUT OF BREATH AND drops into the empty chair next to Kelsey. "I'm famished." She smiles at me. "I'm glad you're here. We need to talk."

"About what?"

"I have an idea."

Lisa clucks her tongue. "Uh-oh, here it comes. The Megan Idea."

Megan leans toward me. "You don't like living on the farm, right?"

I nod, not sure where she's going with this.

Megan sits back and folds her arms. "Then we're going to help you get *off* the farm."

Kelsey snorts. "We are?"

"Think about it, Taylor. What if you could convince your parents that the farm was a mistake? What if you could show them that they'd be happier if you all moved into town?"

I bite into my hamburger. I don't say this out loud,

but if we ever move again, I want our family to move back to Minneapolis, not Melberg. "So, what's your idea?"

"It's called TEFF: Taylor Escapes From Farm."

We all laugh, and I'm suddenly glad my name isn't Jessica. The plan would then be JEFF. "So how does TEFF work?" I ask.

Megan's forehead creases. "I haven't figured that out yet. We need to come up with a plan." She motions to the others. "How can Taylor get off the farm?"

"She could divorce her parents," Lisa says, tossing her bangs out of her eyes. "Then Taylor could live wherever she wants."

Kelsey coughs on her milk. "You want her parents to break up?"

"No, stupid. I want her to find out if she can divorce her parents. Legally, I mean."

Kelsey raises her hand. "Okay, okay. I saw that on Judge Julie. If a kid can support herself financially, she can ask to be emanated . . . no, emancipated, from her parents."

"I don't have any money," I say.

Megan chews her food thoughtfully, and I chuckle to myself. She looks like Pearl chewing her cud. "Then you need to *convince* them to leave," she says.

"It's really nice that you want to help me, but I don't think there's anything anyone can do."

"I've got it!" Megan puts down her sandwich. "Remember when that kid in high school lost his arm a few years ago?"

They nod and my eyes bug out. "You want to cut off my arm?"

"No, silly, listen. The guy caught his arm in some farming thing and it ripped off."

"That's awful," I mutter.

"My uncle knew a guy with a huge scar on his leg from a farm accident," Lisa says.

Kelsey bites into an apple and talks with her mouth full. "My cousin broke his leg when the little tractor he was driving started to tip. He jumped off and his leg got pinned underneath."

I see where they're going with this. "You can get diseases on a farm, like tetanus," I offer.

"Good," Megan says. She pulls out a notebook and writes: *Number One: Farms are dangerous places.* "What else?"

I squint. "I feel trapped out there. I can't drive, and it's too far to bike or walk. I'm all alone."

"Social isolation," Lisa says. "That could really mess you up. I'd go crazy if I couldn't walk downtown or over to Megan's house."

Megan writes *Number Two: Isolation will make you crazy.*

"My parents won't believe I'll go crazy."

"But if you stay on that farm, you'll end up a scary loner," Megan replies. "You won't be normal. You won't be able to get a decent job when you grow up. You'll be ostracized by your peers."

"Ostracized," I say. "That sounds bad." What a life. Discombobulated *and* ostracized.

Lisa smacks the table. "I've got another one. Self-esteem. Teachers are always telling us to develop high self-esteem. But on the farm, you're missing out on life so your self-esteem will suffer."

Megan writes: *Number Three: Farms cause low self-esteem*.

"But how do I convince my parents that farms are dangerous and isolating and mess up self-esteem?"

"Articles," Kelsey says. "Print them off the Internet and leave them around the house."

"Brilliant." Megan and Kelsey knock knuckles while Lisa plays with the end of her ponytail, looking worried.

"That sounds simple enough," I say, "but I'm not sure a few articles will change things."

Megan smiles slyly. "You get good grades, right?"

I shrug. "Yeah, pretty good."

"Ever get a C?"

"No."

"What would your parents do if you started flunking your tests and homework assignments?"

"They'd freak."

"Which is exactly what you want. Low grades," Megan whispers. "That's the secret."

"What?"

"Your grades slip. You start acting depressed. Your

71

parents say 'Taylor, what's wrong?' You say 'I hate school, I hate myself.' You tell them you can't get out of bed in the morning. Your parents will see that being on the farm is bad for you, physically, mentally, socially, and emotionally. They'll stay up late discussing it and will finally decide that this move has been bad for you."

I listen carefully, really flattered they're giving my problem so much attention. But get bad grades on purpose? I can't imagine doing that. My parents would feel terrible. *I'd* feel terrible.

"So, what do you think?" Megan asks.

Lisa zips her lunch bag closed. "I think it's brilliant. It could totally work."

I lick my lips. "I need to think about it."

Megan's gaze is fierce. "No, you need to decide *now*. If this is going to work, we must get started right away."

They're all looking at me. I feel a blotch start up my neck. It's true that I'm tired of animal poop, and I'm tired of Mom and Dad being tired. And both Mom and Dad are starting to keep secrets from each other. That never happened in Minneapolis. Also, I have only one childhood. What if my parents spend it building fences and doing chores?

I meet Megan's gaze. If I say "No," will she drop me from her list of best friends? If I say "Yes," could we actually convince my parents to move? Mom has always wanted to be a farmer but she's worn out all the time. And

72

last Saturday, I overheard Mom and Dad talking late at night. I couldn't hear their words, but their tone sounded very serious. It made me nervous.

I fold up my napkin and toss it on my tray. "I'm in."

CHAPTER FOURTEEN

In math class, Mr. Hickman shows us a DVD about how architects and construction companies use math to design and build houses. It's pretty cool. They use math to make sure the corners are square, that the stairs are all the same height, that the walls are strong enough to bear the weight of the house. Then he gives us an assignment: the class will break into teams of two and each team will design the perfect house. I sit up straight as Mr. Hickman consults his list. "Abel and Donnelly, Frome and Harris . . . Magnuson and McNamara."

I'm being teamed up with Josh. Erk! I would rather wear barn boots or smell like Jersey or be run over by corn-crazed sheep than partner with him.

Mr. Hickman explains each team is to design one house. "Team project," he says. "Two people, one house, one grade."

Josh raises his hand. "Coach, could I—"

Mr. Hickman cuts Josh off. "No changes. Today your job is to make a list of what you want in your house. What requirements must it meet? What sort of life must it support? Everyone find your partner and get started."

I drag myself back to an empty desk beside Josh and sit down with a heavy thump. He opens his notebook and looks kind of excited. I raise an eyebrow.

Josh leans forward. "Megan told me about TEFF. It's a cool idea. I don't blame you for wanting to move."

My mouth drops open. "Why? You've been making fun of me since school started."

He shrugs. "I know, but I get how a farm could be a drag. Luckily the only animals at my house are my dog and my three brothers."

I smile in spite of myself.

"Megan said you need to start getting bad grades. If you follow Megan's advice—act like you won't cooperate—I can complain to Coach Hickman. He'll write you up in your planner since he's all about teamwork."

"Team members get the same grade, so if I get a bad grade, you will too."

Josh shakes his head. His blondish-brown hair is so thick it barely moves. "That's the cool part. You just *pretend*. Then when the assignment is due, you agree to cooperate, and we submit my design. We'll both get As, I'll be able to keep playing football, and you'll still have a black mark in your planner, which is what you want, right?"

I stare at Josh. It can't hurt. "Well, okay. What do we do first?"

"We make a list, like Hickman says. Then I'll design a

house based on the list. You don't have to do anything."

I nod, a little sick to my stomach. It actually sounds like a fun assignment, but thanks to TEFF, I won't be doing it.

We start making a list of what a house should be all about. First on the list is the obvious stuff, like protection from rain, wind, snow, and cold. "A house gives you privacy from neighbors," I say.

Josh writes that down. "I saw a house in Chicago with glass walls. You could see everything that was going on inside. It was weird." He bites the end of his pen. "We want our house to have lots of privacy inside, too. Lots of walls, lots of rooms." He adds that to the list.

"Wait," I say. "Don't you want to have fewer walls and more open space? That way kids and parents can spend more time together."

He looks at me as if I've told him football is a stupid game. "Are you crazy? Why would you want that? Let the parents have their space, and give the kids their own rooms so they can get away from everyone else. You need walls so you can't hear your brothers fighting or your mom talking on the phone all day long."

"But the family that's going to live in this house is so busy. Parents work all day. Kids are in school and then off doing stuff. If everyone hides in their rooms, the family will never spend time together."

Josh glares at his list. "Hickman said we're supposed to write down what we want from a house. I want privacy.

I don't want my family in my face twenty-four-seven."

The bell rings. Class is over. Josh and I stand without speaking. He wants me to pretend to *not* be a team player. Working with him, I may not have to pretend.

CHAPTER FIFTEEN

AFTER SCHOOL I FIND MOM SITTING ON THE PORCH reading a book. I peer over her shoulder at a color photo of something whitish coming out the back end of a sheep. "Erk!" I yell right in Mom's ear.

She laughs and waves me away. "It's just a lamb, silly. See, there's the nose, and those little black things underneath the nose are the two front hooves. When the nose and hooves are lined up like this, the lamb comes right out."

I look closer, then shut my eyes. Too much information. I know the answer but I ask the question anyway. "Why are you reading this?"

"The vet came this afternoon and did an ultrasound. It turns out that both Ruby and Pearl are pregnant, and they're each carrying twins." She's using her *Isn't this exciting!* voice, but her face looks worried. "The lambs could be born any day now."

I sit down on the white wicker chair beside her. "Wow. This is huge." Now I'm worried too. "What are you going to do?"

She holds up the book. "Study this, for one. It has all the information I need. And if I have problems, Dr. Muscato said he'd help me when the time comes. All we have to do is call him."

"We?" I say weakly.

Mom chuckles. "Don't worry. I've been looking forward to this for years, so there's no way I'm going to miss it. You can stay inside and watch a DVD."

"Excellent. But what if I'm the only one home?" As if I don't have enough to worry about with TEFF and all that it might involve.

Mom waves her cell phone. "Call me. My boss said I can leave work if I need to. He used to raise sheep and knows I want to be here when it happens."

"What if the lambs are born at night? Or on a weekend? Will Dr. Muscato still help?"

"Vets come to the farm anytime there's an emergency—day, night, week day, weekend. But if he's busy . . ." She motions to a pink plastic bucket filled with stuff. "I've put together a lambing kit with everything I need."

Inside is a jumble of stuff, including a box of clear plastic gloves. "What are the gloves for?"

"In case I have to reach inside to help deliver the lambs."

I make a face. There's also a bottle of molasses. More bottles of liquids. A box of syringes and needles. Towels. A blue rubber bulb. "What's this bulb for?"

Mom looks up. "You use it to clear fluid from the lamb's nose and mouth to help it breath. Squeeze it first to create a vacuum, then put it up the nose and release it. It's supposed to suck up fluid." I squeeze the bulb, put the open end against my arm, and release the bulb. "Feels funny," I say as it sucks in my skin. I put it back. The bucket's contents don't seem like the stuff you'd need to help deliver a baby.

After eating a snack, slipping on my barn boots, and watching Lost and Found and his siblings paddle around in their pool, I wander into the barn. Mom has put Ruby and Pearl into a pen. I climb into the pen and scratch Ruby's head. I stare at her belly. Are there really babies in there? With both palms pressed against her sides, I hold my breath. Nothing. I can't feel any little kicks, but what do I know?

Before bed I do my homework, but I make sure to get half of the algebra questions wrong. It feels weird. I start an essay for social studies and write four pages. This is twice as many as the teacher asked for, which means I'll get a good grade. Shuddering, I cross out all the good stuff and end up with one page that makes no sense.

CHAPTER SIXTEEN

THE NEXT DAY MEGAN INVITES ME TO HER CASTLE HOUSE after school to work on TEFF. Mom agrees to pick me up at Megan's on her way home from work.

Megan's house is amazing. Warm-looking wood floors. Thick rugs with funky designs. High ceilings with cool carvings in them. Comfortable furniture. There is a fireplace in nearly every room, although most are covered with fancy screens and aren't being used.

Megan waves to an elderly man reading in the living room. "Hi, Gramps, this is my friend Taylor."

Mr. Zink is tall, with large hands like baseball mitts. "Howdy, Taylor. You girls want a snack?"

"Totally," Megan says. "Any suggestions?"

"You got your oranges, you got your grapes, you got your bananas." Megan makes a face. "Or you got your apples and them little cartons of caramel your grandma put out on the counter before she went to her book group."

I barely have time to say thanks before Megan beckons me into the kitchen. "I'm starved," she says, so we cut up apples and grab the containers of caramel. I follow her up two flights of stairs, our footsteps muted by the lush blue carpeting. "Your grandparents live with your family?"

"Yes, they're retired." She snorts. "Guess what they used to do before moving in with us?"

I'm clueless, so I shake my head.

"They raised sheep."

"You're kidding!"

"That's why I came up with TEFF. Farms are okay places to visit, but I wouldn't want to live on one."

Megan's bedroom is all pink. Pink carpet. Pink walls. Pink and green comforter. There's a fireplace with two pink, cushy chairs right next to it. A perfect place to read or spin or just sit and talk. I plop down into the nearest chair as Megan marches to her computer. "Don't get too relaxed. We have work to do."

I dip an apple slice into the caramel. "Can't we hang out for a while?"

Megan begins typing at the keyboard. "Perfect . . . and here's another one . . . Exactly what we need." The printer beside her begins to suck up paper and spit it out.

"Read these articles about social isolation of rural kids."

I staple three articles together, then return to my nest by the fireplace. "This one says that 'rural teens face serious obstacles like social isolation, fewer educational and economic opportunities, and limited access to health care.'"

"That should alarm your parents."

I gape at the next article. "This one's about teen pregnancy."

"That'll make your parents really freak. Leave the articles around the house where your parents can find them."

Megan keeps printing and I keep reading. *Isolation Leads to Teen Suicide. Farming Can Be Dangerous to Your Health. Small Farms are Obsolete. Causes of Middle Grade Low Self-Esteem.* The more I read, the more depressed I get. This stuff is really bad. I'm definitely doing the right thing by getting us off the farm. By now my container is spotless because I've licked out the last of the caramel.

"Okay, your turn at the computer. I want to eat my apple," Megan says. "Search for 'dangers of farm life.'"

I click on the first link, farmfacts.info, and my jaw drops. "Wow."

Each year 100,000 children under the age of 20 are injured or killed on farms.

The farm injury rate is highest for children under the age of 15.

Up to 60% of farm injuries occur when working with livestock.

Megan leans closer to the screen, her apple dripping with caramel. "Perfect. We need to turn these scary statistics into signs you put up around your house, since basically your whole farm is a danger zone."

I open her word processing program and begin typing.

"What do you miss most about your old life?" Megan asks.

I swallow. "Everything."

"I'm not surprised," Megan murmurs. "It's so wrong for parents to drag their kids all over the place like they're luggage or something."

"That's exactly what I feel like—luggage!" I print out the "farm safety" signs.

"Oh, and before I forget," Megan says, "if we're going to get you off the farm, be careful not to hang around farm kids."

"You mean Caleigh?"

"Yes, and anyone else in 4-H."

I blow out a breath. "I don't know—"

"Say 'Yes, Megan.'"

"Yes, Megan," I say.

She grins and stuffs another apple slice into her mouth.

While Megan eats, I click on a few more links. I learn that less than one percent of people in the United States farm. I find this amazing since there's so much food in the grocery stores. Another article says that the number of people who play the online game FarmFanatics outnumber real farmers eighty to one. Wow. People like to play at farming, but they don't like to do it. Considering all the poop involved, I'm not surprised.

An hour later, Mom picks me up. "How was your day?" I ask.

"Long."

We're silent as Mom drives. She's tired again. When

we get home, I stick the farm safety notes on the refrigerator, on the bathroom wall, and in the hallway. Then I put a stack of articles on the kitchen counter, one by the computer in Dad's office, and a few on the coffee table in the living room.

The more I think about TEFF, the more I think it might work.

CHAPTER SEVENTEEN

IT'S SATURDAY AND WE'RE GOING TO VISIT FLORENCE again. "I found an interesting note on the refrigerator," Mom says as she backs out of the garage. "And a pile of rather alarming articles on the kitchen counter."

"Have you read them?"

"A few. Your dad took some to work to read during his lunch break." Mom sighs. "I'm sorry you're so unhappy on this farm. I don't know what we can possibly do."

The obvious answer is "move," but it's too soon to bring that up. I need more demerits in my student planner. "I'm not a piece of luggage, you know."

"What does that mean?"

I shrug. Mom hates shrugging even more than sarcasm. She tries a few more times to get me to talk, but I stay silent.

Florence answers the door in orange jeans that are so loose they almost slip down her hips. She doesn't really have a butt to keep the jeans up. Her turquoise blouse is covered with little orange flowers. She greets us as I carry in the spinning wheel.

"So Ruby and Pearl are pregnant," Florence says. "Very exciting news. May I visit the lambs after they're born?"

"Of course, of course." Mom paces the room like a cougar in a cage. "I hope the lambs are born when I'm home, or that Taylor can call me at work so I can be there. I don't want to miss this."

Florence watches Mom pace. "Don't worry, Kirsten, you'll do fine. You can always call Dr. Muscato, or me, for that matter."

"I appreciate that. I've read the book. I have my lambing box ready, but I'm a little nervous. I've waited so long for baby lambs." She sounds more scared than excited.

Florence motions to the TV. "A new episode of Celebrity Star Stage awaits you."

I whoop and give her a little hug. I thought Mom would sit at the wheel, but she keeps pacing between the kitchen and the living room. "Do you have any coffee?" she asks.

"It's brewing. Look! You've finished all the roving." Florence runs her fingers over the full bobbin.

"Taylor spun it," Mom says. "At first I thought I was losing my mind, then I figured out a little elf was spinning while I was outside fencing or doing chores." She makes a face. "I think there's only one spinner in this family, and it's not me."

"Taylor's found a new hobby," Florence says.

I shrug. "It was something to do."

Florence turns serious. "You are really very good, Taylor. I can tell you have clever hands."

I blotch, embarrassed.

"Some people spend years struggling to spin yarn that looks this nice. But your hands know what to do. That's what I mean by clever hands. You have a light touch. Your hands learn quickly." She sits down at the wheel and moves a full bobbin to a pin at the bottom of the wheel. "Reminds me of myself when Martin and I started raising sheep. He said I had eyes on the tips of my fingers."

Mom chuckles. "Eyes on your fingers?"

"Sometimes, as lambs are being born, they get all mixed up together inside the ewe. So I'd slide my hand inside the ewe and sort everything out." It sounds as if she misses the sheep. "I would close my eyes and let my fingers 'see'—Okay, that's the front leg of one lamb, and that's the head of another."

I frown. "How can you see with your eyes closed?"

"Your other senses grow stronger and your fingers get smart." She runs yarn up through the thingamabob. "Taylor, when you spin, do you watch your hands all the time?"

I try to remember. "No, I guess not."

"Your hands are clever. They learn as they go. They feel the roving so you don't need to watch it. Now let me teach you both the next step. It's easier than spinning. Each of these two bobbins of yarn you've spun is considered a 'ply.'

So if you twist two of them together, what do you have?"

Mom and I look at each other. "Two-ply yarn?" Mom answers. After watching for a few minutes, Mom takes Florence's place at the wheel. After five minutes she stands and shakes out her hands. "I don't think I'm cut out for this. I get so bored, and I can't keep my eyes open. I *don't* have clever hands."

Florence motions to me as Mom wanders into the kitchen for coffee. "Then Taylor shall ply." She gets me started, and it's so easy I can watch TV at the same time, only looking at my hands every five seconds or so. Florence returns to her knitting, a mass of pink and white.

"Do you miss the sheep?" I ask.

Florence sighs but keeps knitting, her needles clicking softly. "Yes, I do. I've been a shepherd for so long that since moving here, I've had a hard time figuring out what I'm supposed to do next." Her hands stop. "It's been difficult adjusting to life in the city."

I bite my lip when Florence calls Melberg a "city."

"But I've agreed to teach spinning and knitting at the Community Center, so I am putting down some new roots. Most of my friends have moved to Arizona, so I need to make new ones."

I'm surprised to hear that even at her age, Florence has the same problem I do.

Mom's cell rings in the kitchen, and I recognize Dad's ringtone. "I'm fine," Mom says. "We're at Florence's. When do you think you'll be home?" Mom's voice is cold, like she's angry. The TV doesn't cover her words. "This is the third weekend you've had to work. Am I supposed to do everything myself?"

"So, Taylor," Florence speaks loudly. "If you're going to spin yarn, you should know something about wool. Any idea what you'd find if you cut open a baseball?"

I try to shut out Mom's voice. "A rubber ball or something."

"A rubber core wrapped with 220 yards of wool yarn." My eyebrows lift.

"A baseball bat is moving at 70 mph when it hits the ball. But does the ball get all squashed out of shape?"

I shake my head, enjoying the feel of the yarn sliding through my hands as I ply it together.

"No, it doesn't. Wool bounces back. It gets whacked out of shape, but then it restores itself."

"Michael, I really need you *here*. I can't manage all by myself." Mom's voice rises even higher.

"Here's something else interesting about wool." Florence's voice is calm. "What do you think is the strongest fiber there is?"

"Silk. We learned that last year."

"It's true, a single strand of silk is strong, but how durable is it? A strand of wool can be bent more than 20,000 times without breaking, Cotton breaks after 3,000 bends, and silk collapses after only 1,800. Isn't that amazing? Wool is resilient. Do you know what that means?"

I nod, scared now by Mom's voice in the kitchen. She's

having a meltdown. I hear a cell phone smack against the table.

"Resilience means to bounce back, to stand back up after getting knocked down." Florence smiles at me. "Keep plying, Taylor. You're making real yarn now. When you finish plying at home, wrap the yarn around and around the back of a chair until you have a nice, big skein of yarn. Then soak the yarn in lukewarm water and hang it up to dry. Hang something heavy from the yarn, like a sneaker or a can of paint. The weight will straighten out all the twists. Bring it back, and we'll dye it."

I nod again. Mom comes out of the kitchen. "Thank you so much for the lesson," she says, "but I think Taylor and I should be going."

I want to ask Mom if I can stay longer. It's quiet at Florence's. There's TV. And no anger. Instead, I pick up the spinning wheel. Florence gives me a funny look, like she wants to say something, but she just pats my shoulder. She walks us to the door and invites us to come back anytime.

CHAPTER EIGHTEEN

AFTER MONDAY'S ENGLISH CLASS, I SEE CALEIGH IN the crowded hallway with a bunch of kids in 4-H jackets. They're gathered around a girl with a white, fuzzy rabbit in her arms. Beyond this group, Megan and Lisa are talking at Lisa's locker. My heart sinks. Megan wants me to avoid Caleigh, but I need to walk down the hallway to get to math class.

"Hey, Taylor!" Caleigh calls. "Come see Lucy's rabbit. It's the softest thing on the planet."

Megan looks in my direction, and she sees Caleigh's group. My brain spins. Think of something to say as you pass. Don't stop and pet the rabbit. Say something like, "Cute bunny, no time to talk." Or "Can't stop. Will explain later."

But my brain doesn't move as quickly as my feet. Suddenly I've walked right by Caleigh without saying a word. I'm so busy trying to think of what to say that I don't even look at her. Flustered, I stop at Lisa's locker.

"Very smooth," Megan says.

Lisa nods as she closes her locker. "Totally icy."

They are complimenting me, so I should feel good.

But I don't.

In math class we split up into teams again. Josh and I watch the other teams bend their heads together, and I try not to think about how I ignored Caleigh in front of all her friends. The room buzzes with words like *roof* and *kitchen* and *closet*.

I open my notebook and begin doodling. I draw big loopy circles across the page. An image starts forming in my mind.

Circles. Houses. Hey, an idea! I lean forward. "We could design a round house."

"That's the stupidest thing I've ever heard." Josh opens his notebook. "I've designed the perfect house, so you don't have to do anything. When it gets close to the due date, and I've complained to Coach that you aren't cooperating, then we'll submit this design."

"Let me see." It looks like a series of rooms stacked on top of each other. "I don't get it."

"This is the first floor. Kitchen and parents' bedroom and bathroom. This house has a small—what did Coach call it?—a small footprint." He points to the next box stacked on top of the first. "This is the second floor where the two youngest brothers live. Then on top of that is the third floor, where the next brother lives. And the fourth floor is where the oldest brother lives. He gets to sleep and eat and watch TV up there by himself."

"That's a dumb house. You'll need too many stairs."
I draw a circle on my page. "Here's a better idea. A round
house. The bedrooms and bathrooms are built along the
back part of the circle. They all open into the middle. The
center of the house is where everything happens—kitchen,
dining room, family room." Excited now, I sketch in walls
coming out from the circle's edge. "You wouldn't need
to waste space with hallways because the rooms are right
there."

Josh taps my paper with his pen and snorts as if I'm
the lamest person he's ever known. "Still stupid. There's no
way to get away from the other people."

"That's the point," I snap. "The whole family is together.
They eat together, watch TV together, and are close in case
anyone needs anything." I draw a small circle in the center of the round house. "This is House Central, a big table
where the family eats and pays bills and does homework.
You could have outlets in it for laptops and games could be
stored underneath."

"No, no, no. We're not designing a round house. Forget it."

I consider our two plans. "Round is better. Cozier. Your
house sticks way up in the air. Mine hugs the ground."

"Yours takes up too much land."

"And yours isn't a house, it's a stack of apartments."

I begin another round floor plan, carefully labeling
each room and each closet while Josh scribbles a floor plan
for his stupid boxes. We work in silence, each determined

to come up with the better plan, when Mr. Hickman suddenly appears.

"I don't see much teamwork going on here. How well you work together will be half your grade."

Josh gives me a significant look. "Coach, don't you always say that teamwork is about give and take, about compromise?" The teacher nods. "Maybe you should give that lecture to Boots," Josh says. I know he's trying to help, but he's also mad because I don't like his house plan. "She won't compromise."

"Teamwork is different with every team, Magnuson. Figure out how to work together. I see an F in your future if you don't."

An F? My tongue sticks to the roof of my mouth.

"Coach, I can't play football with an F."

"Then follow the assignment. Two people. One house. End of story." He stares at my paper, then at Josh's. "Make the design less gender specific."

"Huh?" Josh looks confused.

"The round house? Clearly designed by a girl." I gasp. My house plan looks like a breast. Mr. Hickman taps Josh's paper. "And the tall house jutting into the sky? Designed by a boy." Josh gives a strangled cry and turns bright red. I blotch like I've never blotched before.

Horrified, I keep my eyes on my paper as Mr. Hickman walks away. The only thing that stops me from totally melting into my chair is the bell.

CHAPTER NINETEEN

THE NEXT MORNING I HEAD FOR THE CHICKEN HOUSE with my umbrella. The chickens are pecking around outside, however, so I don't need it. I check each nest box, finding more eggs than usual. Maybe I'll beat my record. When I get to the end of the row of nest boxes, my boot bumps against something on the ground. I yelp and jump back. It's a dead chicken, the pebbly skin on its legs nearly white. I cry out when I recognize the golden feathers. No, no, no!

I step closer. Yes, it's Butterscotch. I run out the door and slam it behind me. I close my eyes as I lean against the building.

Choking back tears, I call Mom but she doesn't answer. I call Dad and he picks up. "Hey, Tay. What's up?"

"Butterscotch is dead!"

"Butterscotch? The chicken?"

"Yes," I cry. "I don't know what happened. She's lying on the ground. I don't know what to do."

"Honey, you need to calm down. These things happen.

Hens don't live a long time, and she was probably pretty old anyway."

"Is that supposed to make me feel better?"

"No, I guess not." He clears his throat, sounding as if he'd rather be in a meeting than talking to me about a dead chicken. "You're going to have to pick it up, put it in one of those empty paper feedbags, and stick it in the trash."

"*It?* Her name is Butterscotch."

"Sorry. You'll need to put her in the trash."

"I *can't*."

"You need to, honey. I'm gone until after supper tonight, and your mom . . . she'll be tired when she gets home from work."

I hang up. It's wrong to throw Butterscotch away. She was my favorite hen. I put on gloves and return to the chicken house. I pick her up by one leg, but she feels so stiff and weird that I drop her immediately. I loved the live Butterscotch, but I can't bear to touch the dead one. Her eyes are closed, and her lids look as pebbly as her legs. I try again, telling myself I should be able to do this.

But I just can't. I finally use a shovel to scoop Butterscotch into the feedbag and roll it closed, saying over and over again, "I'm sorry, I'm sorry."

I check the time. The bus will be here soon, but I don't care. I get a shovel from the garage and walk around the house to the backyard. I begin to dig a hole under the huge oak tree I can see from my bedroom window. The clay soil is heavy, but it comes loose in big clumps when I dig. I place Butterscotch in the hole, wiping my nose and eyes, then cover her up.

The bus is late, so I have time to put the shovel away, change out of my boots, and wait at the end of the driveway. I want to sit next to Caleigh and tell her about Butterscotch, but she's sitting with someone else. Besides, I humiliated her yesterday in front of her friends. I'm probably the last person she wants to see.

I go through the day in a fog. I smile and nod at all the right times, but I can't believe how sad I feel.

I beat Mom home, but not by much. When she drives into the driveway, I'm sitting on the porch. She climbs the short steps and gives me a half hug. She leans back. "What's wrong?"

I press my lips together. "I found Butterscotch dead this morning."

Mom slumps into the chair beside me.

My eyes fill up and my throat feels tight. "I called you, but you didn't answer. Then I called Dad and he told me to stick her in the garbage. In the *garbage*, Mom. Really. How awful is that?"

Mom pats my arm, but she's not really paying attention. "Another dead chicken," she whispers.

Later, after we finish eating pasta and vegetables, I scrape the dishes. "Hey, Mom, want to have some ice cream on the porch?"

"I have to finish repairing the north fence, Taylor. Sorry."

"Can't you *ever* take a break?"

"Dad has to work late again, and I can't move the sheep to fresh pasture until I get that fence fixed. It's a mess. I'll be in after dark."

I finish the dishes and go outside. All I can think about is Butterscotch.

I pass the duck family resting in the shade under a tree, and I'm happy to see that Lost and Found is napping with them. I hang out with Ruby and Pearl in the barn for a while. I stare at their sides, watching for a kick or some sign of life. Nothing.

After an hour of wasting time with the sheep, I leave the barn. Mom's down in the pasture banging metal fence posts into the ground with a post pounder. The sound of metal ringing on metal isn't pretty.

As I walk toward the house, I see something on the ground at the edge of the driveway. It's a pile of yellow feathers fluttering in the breeze. A duckling. "No, no." I run closer. There's a little brown spot on the yellow head. It's Lost and Found.

The body is in one piece, but there are specks of blood on his neck. Something killed him. He's dead. I drop to my knees and pick up his little body. His feathers are so soft.

Two deaths in one day. It's just too much. I stare at Lost and Found through my tears. What am I supposed to do? Put him in a bag and throw him into the trash like Dad wanted me to do with Butterscotch? After wiping my wet face, I find a small metal box on one of the garage shelves and line it with a paper towel. I gently settle Lost and Found in the box and stroke his chest one more time.

I dig a small hole next to Butterscotch. I place the box in the hole, then refill it, tucking the clay soil around the box like a blanket.

Exhausted, I sit down on the grass and really lose it. *Both* Butterscotch and Lost and Found? How can death happen so quickly? One minute Lost and Found is fine. The next minute he's dead. Why him? What could I have done to prevent it? He was an adventurer, and short of putting him into a cage, I couldn't have changed that. I've experienced more death in one day on this farm than in twelve years in Minneapolis. This farming life is crazy. And painful. And stupid. Everything dies, at least everything I care about.

I wipe my eyes with my sleeve. This is horrible. Just horrible. I've lost two animals with names. What about Ruby and Pearl? Will they die too?

Inside the house, I climb up the narrow staircase to my bedroom. The "Bloom Where You're Planted" T-shirt is draped across the back of my chair.

I don't want Megan's TEFF plan to take months. I don't want it to take weeks. I want it to succeed in days. Bad grades aren't enough. I pull my student handbook off my shelf. It's full of rules just waiting for me to break. I'm going to create a tornado of troubles. A blizzard of badness. I make a list of ways to get demerits, since I must get off this farm before something else dies.

Dusk settles over the house and the cool air forces me to close my window. I sit on my bed and fantasize again about running away or being adopted.

Yesterday the population of the McNamara farm was seventy-six. Now it's seventy-four. If I succeed, by Thanksgiving the farm population will fall to exactly zero.

CHAPTER TWENTY

On my way from Team Time to English class the next day, I take off my hoodie. I'm wearing such a short top that my midriff shows.

In English, Ms. Benton asks us to pass our assignments forward. I don't turn anything in. When Ms. Benton begins a lecture on suffixes, a question occurs to me. I would usually wait until after class to ask a question unrelated to the teacher's lecture, but now I'm Taylor on a mission. I'm totally dedicated to TEFF. I raise my hand.

"Ms. Benton, I have a question about prefixes."

"We'll get to those in our next class."

"It's about the "dis" prefix. It usually makes sense. The opposite of disengage is engage. The opposite of distrust is trust."

My teacher, short and lean like a runner, sets her jaw. "Ms. McNamara, your question—"

"But then things get weird. What about disease? Is the opposite word ease? And what's the opposite of discuss? Cuss?"

The class starts laughing.

"That's enough, Taylor."

"My biggest confusion, however, is discombobulate." My heart's really pounding now. It's scary, but also a little fun to be someone other than who I usually am. "It means bewildered, bedeviled, befuddled, bemused, befogged."

The laughter continues.

"Taylor, we'll return to prefixes—"

"But what's the opposite of discombobulate? Combobulate? Bobulate?"

"Taylor, you're about to get a demerit for disrupting class."

"There's another one—disrupt. If I stop *dis*rupting class, then am I *rupting* class?"

Ms. Benton ignores the laughter as she writes in my planner, then gives me a hall pass to the principal's office. But I take a detour and hide in the bathroom, half excited, half-horrified, until the bell rings.

In science I totally blow the multiple-choice quiz. I know each answer, but I choose the answer above or below it. Mr. Rashid looks at my bare midriff but doesn't say anything. Two other teachers, however, tell me to change into something more appropriate.

Maybourne doesn't hear about my dress code violation until after lunch. He tracks me down in social studies. He walks in without apologizing, asks for my planner, and writes me up. With a stern glance meant to show that he's serious, he hands back the planner. "I will be calling your parents." He tells me to stop in the office between classes and find a more suitable shirt in the Lost and Found, which now has clothing in it. I don't do it. The only Lost and Found box I care about is buried under an oak tree in my backyard.

Mom arrives home at the same time I get off the bus. She asks how my day went, and for a second I think Maybourne's already talked to her, but she changes into her chore clothes. "I'm going to check on Ruby. Last night her udder looked even fuller than the day before. It won't be much longer now."

"Are you excited?" I ask. "This is what you've always wanted, right? Baby lambs."

Her smile is weak. "Sure, I'm excited. Can't wait."

I don't know what to say. Parents are supposed to reassure kids, not the other way around. Besides, the way things have been going on this farm, I wouldn't be surprised if something did go wrong.

After she leaves, I check the answering machine and delete a message from Maybourne. Just after I do that, Mom's cell rings. She's left it in the kitchen. After it stops ringing, I wait a few minutes, then delete the message Maybourne has left. This is not Taylor behavior. It's Taylor-Escapes-From-Farm behavior. Go TEFF.

It's amazing how much time you have when you don't do any homework. I finish plying all the yarn and wrap it around and around the back of a wide chair until I have a big skein. I follow Florence's directions, and soon the skein is hanging from a hanger in the laundry room, with Dad's old sneaker pulling it down to straighten it.

That night I wake up to my parents' voices downstairs. They sound tense and angry. "You've got to help me more, Michael."

"Kirsten, I'm doing the best I can. But someone has to make enough money to feed all these animals."

"You're using your job as an excuse to avoid being here."

The argument goes on and on. I've never heard them fight like this before. I pull the covers over my head, but it doesn't help. I close my door, but that doesn't help either. I slip into the upstairs bathroom and find two cotton balls. I tiptoe back to bed and jam the cotton into my ears. It shuts out the voices. Unfortunately it doesn't shut out the sound of the front door slamming.

That week I get my English paper back. D. I get my media class quiz back. D. I get my social studies essay back. D. I take a math test and know I failed it. I delete a few more messages from the home answering machine. Maybourne sounds concerned and wants to talk with my parents before "Taylor gets too far off track." My planner begins to fill with notes from teachers about missed assignments and attitude problems. I forge Mom's signature again.

After having such bad luck with animals, I get lucky in other ways. Sunday Mom loses her cell phone in the pasture and won't have time to buy a new one until later in the week. Monday Dad forgets to take his phone to work. When I get home from school, his cell is in the kitchen, beeping with a message from Maybourne. I delete it. Between the farm and their jobs and the pregnant sheep, Mom and Dad aren't paying much attention to me. That's perfect. But I know this won't last forever. Maybourne will connect with one of my parents soon.

That night Dad comes home before I'm asleep. He gives me a big hug. "School going well?"

"Nope," I say. "It's going really badly. I hate it. My grades stink. I've accumulated almost fifteen demerits. I'm this close to being kicked out."

Dad laughs. "I love your sense of humor." For the first time, he doesn't recognize my sarcasm.

When I wear another short top and short skirt the next day, even Mr. Suarez gets angry. He personally escorts me to the office and waits while I change into an over-sized Minnesota Vikings t-shirt and the same pair of giant sweats I'd worn before. Mr. Suarez no longer looks at me every morning with amusement, wondering what funny farm disaster I've brought to school. Now he looks at me with sad eyes, wondering what rule I'll break next.

CHAPTER TWENTY✳ONE

THE HOUSE PROJECT IS DUE TODAY IN MATH CLASS. JOSH and I stare at each other. "I've changed my mind. I think we should use my circular house," I say.

"No, we agreed to use *my* design. That's the deal we made. You're supposed to be cooperative at the last minute."

I shake my head.

Josh grits his teeth. "Because you won't compromise, I'm gonna get benched. That's not fair."

"You won't compromise either. You won't agree to my round house." Josh flushes. We both know his friends will harass him for designing a house shaped like a breast. "What's the matter?" I ask. "Feeling discom*boob*ulated?" Now he's beet red and I feel awful. He tried to tell me I had chicken poop in my hair. He wanted to help with TEFF. And now I'm sitting here making fun of him.

Mr. Hickman stops by our desks to pick up our final design. We hand him two designs—Josh's tower and my circle—instead of one. Hickman shakes his head and looks at Josh. "The defensive line is going to miss you, dude."

The bell rings and I leap to my feet. I flee down the hallway and tuck myself into a corner to escape the noise. I call Florence, plugging my free ear shut to hear better.

"Hi, Taylor! How's the plying going?"

"I've finished, and school is cancelled for the rest of the day. Something about asbestos. May I come hang out with you?"

"Absolutely. Too bad you don't have your yarn. We could dye it today."

"It's in my locker. I'll get it and be right there." My new rule: Always plan ahead when it comes to skipping school. While the halls are still full, I dash to my locker and grab the bag of yarn. As the hallways empty before the bell, I slip out the front door. I run across the street and around the corner until I'm out of sight of the school windows. My lungs hurt as I walk as fast as I can, almost jogging, until I'm three blocks from school. Skipping school is worth many demerits.

Florence is wearing purple sweats. She gives me a big hug. "Taylor, what a delight. Let's see your yarn."

I open the bag. "I followed your instructions for setting the twist."

She pulls a handful of yarn from the bag. "Taylor, this is lovely. It has character and depth. It will be wonderful to knit." She hands me the bag.

"Let's get started. I'm dying to dye," Florence says,

winking at me. We heat water on the stove and in the microwave. Florence dumps packages of Kool-Aid on the counter. "Okay, Taylor, pick your colors."

I stare at the Kool-Aid. "We're dying yarn with Kool-Aid?"

"It's the easiest way. The colors won't be exactly the name of the flavor, of course, but close enough."

I pick out Blueberry, Lime, and Orange.

We add one package of Kool-Aid to each pot. I carefully lower a skein of white yarn into each color.

"Make sure you don't agitate the yarn. Wool has little barbs, you know, so under pressure all those barbs stick together like one big family, and then you've got felt. Felt's not bad if that's what you want, but you don't want felt. You want yarn." I like the image of the little yarn fibers sticking together like a family, but I'm careful not to "agitate."

While we wait for the dye to work, Florence makes chicken salad sandwiches on white bread cut into little triangles for our lunch. She also makes cucumber sandwiches, which I think will be awful but are really nummy.

Florence wipes her mouth after eating the last of her sandwich. "Are you excited about the babies coming?"

"Mom's got a pink bucket all ready for lambing. I'm planning to hide under my bed when it happens."

Florence laughs. "Oh, no. You'll want to be right there. You never know what's going to happen. Most of the time those lambs just slide right out. One time, though, triplets got so tangled inside I thought I was going to scream. One was coming backwards. The other two were trying to get out at the same time, but—" I cover my ears and she stops. "Oh, dear. That's not the sort of story you want to hear, is it?"

"Not really." To change the subject, I check the dye pots and yelp. "The color's all gone! The water is clear."

Florence looks over my shoulder. "That means the yarn has soaked up all the dye."

We rinse each skein of yarn in the sink. "Now into the microwave," Florence says. "Five minutes for each skein helps set the dye."

When the yarn is finally done, one skein comes out a soft, light blueberry. The lime and orange skeins are brighter.

"Let's put them in plastic bags. You can take them home and hang them up to dry, with shoes hanging on them again for weight. Then you'll be ready to knit."

"I don't know how to knit."

Florence pulls needles and yarn from a bag in her living room. "Then you're going to learn to knit a scarf. Needle in, wrap the yarn like this, needle under and out. Now you try."

She laughs as I follow instructions and end up with everything sliding off the needle. "I think I need more lessons."

"Don't worry. Knitting is more complex than spinning, and the needles take some getting used to." Florence slows down and does it again and again until I'm able to follow her.

"Keep practicing," she recommends. Her phone rings.

I feel lighter than I have in days as I sit in the apartment and focus on the knitting needles. Florence talks quietly in the kitchen and I fantasize about knitting my own sweater some day.

But when Florence comes back and sits down on the sofa beside me, phone in her hand, my spirits sink. Her eyes are angry and her jaw is tight. "It's your mother."

I hold my breath for a second, then blow it out. Busted. *Really* busted.

Florence's voice is flat, and she's not smiling. "They've been looking for you. The school didn't know if you'd cut classes, or had been kidnapped, or what."

My heart nearly pounds its way out of my chest. "I'm sorry I lied to you. I had to get away." I put down the knitting. "I just like being here." She says nothing, but hands me the phone.

"Taylor McNamara, do you have any idea what you've done?" Mom's voice is shaking.

"I'm sorry."

"Dad left work early to help me find you. He's coming to pick you up and bring you back to school. Then we all get to have a meeting in the principal's office to discuss your failing grades and multiple demerits. Won't *that* be special?"

Now I know who I get my sarcasm from.

CHAPTER TWENTY✦TWO

Dad says nothing when I get into the car. His eyes look so sad. While Dad parks in the visitor spot, Mr. Maybourne and Mom wait at the curb. Maybourne looks pleased. Mom wears a look I've never seen before—more shocked and confused than angry. "I found out where your mother works," Maybourne says. "Shall we all step into my office?"

Kids at their lockers stare. Whispers run up and down the hallway. I try not to blotch, but I do anyway. This is the moment I've been looking forward to. But somehow I don't feel so good.

We all four squeeze into Maybourne's office. Mom and Dad sit on chairs, and Maybourne drags in a stool for me. Then Maybourne explains everything I've been doing. He shows them my student planner with all the demerits and missing assignments. He shows them a current list of my grades.

Dad flips through my student planner, his face growing red. A little vein sticks out on his forehead. Mom's face is totally white except for two spots of red on her cheeks. She keeps swallowing, like there's something stuck in her throat.

"There is no excuse for grades like this," Dad says, slamming the planner shut. "You can get As with your eyes closed."

"I cannot believe you forged my signature," Mom says. "I assumed you were old enough to monitor your own schoolwork. I've been distracted, and as a result everyone thinks you're a bad student."

My face heats up. "So what? I don't like living here anyway," I snap. "It's not who I am." And it's not you either, I want to add, but they'd only deny it. Parents hate to admit mistakes, and moving here has been a big one.

Dad rubs his forehead. "We know you weren't wild about the move, but you seemed willing to try. You've collected eggs and helped with other chores. We've been on the farm only two months. It takes longer than that to adjust."

"Two months is long enough," I say.

Maybourne clears his throat. "I'd like to recommend that Taylor see our school counselor twice a week to get back on track."

Dad looks at Mom, incredulous. "Can you believe that? Taylor? Needing a counselor?"

Mom clears her throat. "Mr. Maybourne, we are very sorry about all of this." She glares at me. "Things are going to change immediately. Taylor will be grounded until she makes up all her missed assignments. No staying after school to visit friends. No doing chores, no hanging out with Pearl and Ruby."

I shrug.

Dad squeezes his hands together so tightly his knuckles turn white. "No game nights, no shopping at the Mall of America, no fun of any kind."

I clench my jaw. "You've just described my life, so big deal."

Mom crosses her arms. "You will show us your completed assignments every night before you go to bed."

"You're never available," I say. "You're too busy fixing fences, and Dad's always working in Minneapolis."

Mom looks as if I've slapped her, and my stomach flips over.

Dad turns to Mr. Maybourne. "I spoke with my boss today. I'm going to work at home part-time for the next few weeks so I can help supervise Taylor."

"Why didn't you do that before now," I ask, "when Mom needed your help?"

Mom and Dad look ready to explode so I shut up. They agree I should see the counselor, then they thank Maybourne, shake his hand, and we leave.

None of us says a word as Dad starts the engine. After five minutes I can't take the silence any longer. "We should sell the farm and move back to Minneapolis."

Mom whirls around to glare at me. "Is that why you did this? Hoping we'd give up? We're not going to tuck our tails between our legs and run home that easily."

Does Mom notice that even *she* refers to Minneapolis as home? Dad doesn't say anything.

Dad drives the car into the garage and shuts off the engine. We sit there in silence. "We're very disappointed in you, Taylor," Mom says. "That you would use your schoolwork and behavior to manipulate us into leaving this farm horrifies me. I don't even know who you are anymore."

I leap from the car. At first I run toward the house but I stop. I don't know what to do. Going into that old house where I'm doomed to spend the rest of my childhood is the last thing I want to do. I run to the end of the driveway. I feel full of something I can't name. Whatever it is, it makes me want to keep walking, or kick in a wall, or throw something. I feel like hot oil is boiling up inside of me.

"Taylor, where are you going?" Dad calls.

I stomp up to the skinny house at the end of the driveway and push against it as hard as I can. The ground at the base of the tilting shelter shifts a little. I press my back against the house and push harder.

"Taylor!"

I breathe hard and grunt as the shelter moves. I rock it back and forth until it hovers for a second on its edge. With an angry growl, I shove the whole thing over. It falls into the ditch and cracks into three long pieces.

CHAPTER TWENTY*THREE

MY PARENTS KEEP ME HOME THURSDAY AND FRIDAY, standing over me like jailers until I finish most of my missed assignments. These are not very fun days. Mom and Dad barely talk to each other, let alone me.

Saturday the weather turns warm enough that I can sit outside on the porch. Dried leaves skitter across the driveway, and the ducklings chase them back and forth.

Inside, the phone rings and Mom answers it. "Hi, Janine, thanks for calling me back. Yes, you heard my earlier message correctly. We want to list the farm for sale."

My head snaps up. *What?*

"Yes, I know we might lose money selling so soon, but we've made our decision. If you could stop by this afternoon, we'd appreciate it. Michael and Taylor will be moving back to Minneapolis within the week, and I'll remain here, selling off the animals and cleaning the house." She hangs up.

I can't speak.

Megan got me started with the articles and the bad

grades, but with my demerits, I've finally succeeded in getting my family to move. Something hot and shameful washes over me. I feel sick to my stomach.

I find Mom in the kitchen. "I heard your half of the phone conversation," I say.

She's loading the dishwasher. "You should celebrate. You're going to get what you want."

It's like she punched me in the stomach. I open my mouth to speak but nothing comes out.

Dad appears in the doorway. "Your mom and I have talked about it the last two nights, and we've decided that this farm might have been a mistake."

"Because of me."

"Because of your grades and your alarming behavior, and because of me having to commute hours every day, and all the other things that have gone wrong."

Mom shrugs. "Running a farm is more work than I expected. For the last week I've wished that I could sleep for a month. Then with you skipping, and . . . Well, enough is enough."

I spend most of the day in my room. Dad brings down four empty boxes from the attic and tells me to start packing. I can hear the conversation between Janine the realtor and my parents when Janine comes over. I hear Mom calling area farmers as she tries to sell the animals. The phone rings all afternoon as people call back to ask questions about the goats, the sheep, and the ducks.

Late in the afternoon, I finally answer the twenty texts

Megan sent, asking what happened in Maybourne's office. I text her back that TEFF worked, and that we're moving back to Minneapolis. I think about texting Lauren but don't really feel like it.

In less than a minute, my phone rings. "What went wrong?" Megan yells in my ear. "I thought you'd end up moving to Melberg."

"No, we're moving back to Minneapolis."

"But no one wants you to leave."

"Thanks for everything, Megan." I hang up.

I feel badly that Josh is going to get benched because of me, so I draw a new floor plan for the math assignment. This time I replace the big center table with a circular staircase. The staircase leads up to a tower with one bedroom, and more stairs lead up to another bedroom, and finally to a third. Then I make another copy of the plan. I put one copy into an envelope and address it to Mr. Hickman at school. It's a compromise plan—a round house with a tower of privacy. I put the other copy in an envelope addressed to Josh Magnuson.

I call Florence but she doesn't answer. I leave a message apologizing again for lying about why I wasn't in school.

That evening Dad sets up the ladder next to the house so he can repair a window screen on the second floor. Janine says the house will sell more easily if nothing looks broken.

Holding my umbrella, I collect eggs in the evening,

and find myself talking to the hens. They're inside because chickens like to tuck themselves into bed before dark. In the barn, I climb into the pen with Ruby and Pearl. Pearl runs over to nibble some grain from my palm. "Not many more treats," I tell Pearl. "We're leaving. Hey, Ruby, want a treat?"

Ruby, however, stands in the far corner of the pen, pawing at the straw, bleating softly. I watch her turn around in a circle. Oh no! Something is coming out her back end. I gasp. It's like a red water balloon that's hanging by a thread of fluid. Erk!

I race from the barn. "Mom! Dad!" At the same time an ambulance screams down the gravel road. Lights flashing, the ambulance turns into our driveway. I stop, stunned, my brain frozen. "What? What?"

"Over here!" Mom appears from behind the house, waving to the emergency crew. Two women grab boxes and a stretcher and head for Mom. Heart pounding, I race behind them.

CHAPTER TWENTY✷FOUR

MOM WAVES THE EMTs OVER TO THE SIDE OF THE house. "He was repairing a window when he fell off the ladder and hit his head on this stump. He knocked himself out and now he's really groggy."

I gasp. Dad sits on the ground pressing a bloody cloth to his head.

Mom holds out her arms and I snuggle into her side as one EMT takes Dad's pulse and blood pressure. The other flicks a light into his eyes and examines the cut on his head. "You might have a concussion, so we need to bring you in." She moves the stretcher closer.

I squeeze Mom's hand and she looks down at me, eyes moist. "He's going to be fine. Don't worry. We'll both ride with him in the ambulance."

"Mom, I was in the sheep pen with Ruby just now and saw something coming out of her back end. It looks like a water balloon."

Mom's eyes widen.

"That's the water bag," one of the EMTs says. "If

Ruby's a sheep, you're going to have lambs in an hour or so."

Mom clutches her head. "No! No! This can't be happening." She looks from Dad to me, and then to the barn. She moans, pressing her hands against her eyes. "Okay, okay, don't panic. We can do this. Taylor, call Dr. Muscato. I need you to stay here and wait for him."

"But—"

"He'll come right over. It'll be fine. Your dad and I won't be gone long. The doctor will stitch him right up and we'll be home in less than an hour." I catch the look the two EMTs give each other. The one who climbs into the back of the ambulance motions to Mom, who gives me a quick hug. "I'll be right back, honey. Don't panic. It's going to be fine." She keeps saying that as she climbs in beside Dad. Her face is white and I can see she's really scared.

I swallow hard. "Don't panic. It's going to be fine," I echo as the ambulance disappears down the road, its red taillights glowing in the dusk. The sound of tires on gravel fades fast. Hands shaking, I call the vet.

"Hello, you've—"

"Dr. Muscato, it's Taylor McNamara. We—"

"—reached the phone of Dr. Jeff Muscato. I'm currently on a farm call, so please leave a message and I'll call you back." I stare in horror at my phone. *What?*

I hear the beep so leave a message. "Please come as quickly as you can."

I hang up, stunned. He said he'd come. I call Mom, who can barely hear me in the ambulance.

"Don't worry. He's out at another farm. You have time." Mom's voice, despite her words, is rushed and high-pitched. "Honey, I'm so sorry. This is not how I'd planned this. But your dad is more important than a sheep. I've got to make sure he's okay."

"I know," I choke out, then hang up. I run back into the barn. The water bag's gone now, so it must have dropped into the straw.

I pace until I think I'll scream, then I call Dr. Muscato and get the same message. "It's Taylor McNamara again. The water bag is out, so we really need you. Don't even bother to call. Just come right now, *please*."

An hour later, still no Dr. Muscato. I try not to panic, but in my Home Alone class last year, they taught us how to handle every emergency possible except a sheep going into labor.

Maybe I could call Dr. Muscato's home phone. I run to the house and find Jeffrey Muscato in the phone book, but I get an answering machine. I call two other vets but they either do only cats and dogs, or don't answer. Totally out of ideas, I call Megan and explain. "Your grandfather knows about sheep. Could he come help me?"

Megan sighs. "He's playing Bingo at the VFW tonight."

"Can't you call his cell?"

"It's Bingo. There's loud music, and people yelling

'bingo.' It's insane and he always turns off his phone when he's there."

I stand in the kitchen, staring stupidly at the phone. I run back to the barn. Now something's poking out from Ruby, but I don't know what it is. Obviously part of a lamb, but what part? The nose? And how long is this supposed to take? The EMT said an hour or two. I check my watch. It's been almost two hours and the lamb isn't out. Something's wrong.

I call Mom again. "How's Dad?"

"They're doing a few more tests. He's more alert, but they're worried about the results of the CAT scan." Her voice is tight. "Is Dr. Muscato there yet?"

"He's not answering his phone, and I can't find another vet."

"Shoot. Muscato must have lots of emergencies tonight. He has to take them in the order they come, and he'll do all the dairy cows first because they're so valuable. You should take a minute to scan through my book on lambing. Honey, I'm so sorry, but the doctor's here. Will you be okay?"

I want to scream, "No!" but instead I say "yes" and hang up. I flip through Mom's book, but at every photo I yelp and turn the page. I don't want to know any of this.

I pace the kitchen, then call Caleigh. "Oh thank god," I yell when she answers. "You're home! I need help. Ruby's gone into labor and Mom's at the hospital and the vet's not answering his phone. Can you come?"

"Taylor, calm down. I'm home alone so no one can drive me." Caleigh lives over three miles down the gravel road. "Why don't you call Florence?"

I smack my forehead. "Of course! I've been so freaked I haven't been thinking straight. Thanks!"

Florence answers on the first ring and I almost cry. I explain the situation. "Can you come help?"

"Oh, honey, I'm not even in Melberg. I'm at my niece's in Wisconsin. We're at a musical and I turned on my phone during intermission for messages. But I can talk. You say you see a nose coming out but nothing else?"

"I think so."

"You've got one of two problems. One possibility is that the lamb's front legs are bent under, sort of hung up under the doorway. You need to put on a clear plastic glove, then reach inside and straighten out the legs to make sure they're pointed toward the doorway."

"Reach inside?" I'm having trouble breathing.

"The other possible problem could be that the lamb's front legs are both locked on either side of the doorway, like the lamb doesn't want to come out. You need to convince those little hooves to unlock and get themselves into the doorway. The ewe will do the rest."

"Florence, I don't know if—"

"Remember I said you had clever hands? You can do this, Taylor. Close your eyes. Imagine you can see with your fingers. Feel around and figure out what's going on."

Florence gives me a few more tips, says more encouraging words, and that she's driving home tomorrow. "You'll do great, Taylor."

I thank her and hang up. Someone must help Ruby's lambs. And unless the vet suddenly roars up in his truck, that someone must be me.

CHAPTER TWENTY★FIVE

WITH A BAG OF OLD TOWELS IN ONE HAND AND MOM'S bucket of supplies in the other, I march out into the chilly night wearing my overalls and one of Mom's heavy sweatshirts. I turn on all the lights in the barn, thinking that it'll make me feel braver. Ruby stands in her pen, pawing at the straw. Pearl's in the other corner, chewing her cud.

I climb into the pen and kneel in the straw behind Ruby. This is ridiculous. There's no way I can do this. I hold my breath, listening for the sound of tires on the gravel driveway, for the sound of a car coming down the road.

Nothing. No Mom and Dad. No Dr. Muscato.

I pull on one of the thin plastic gloves. It's so long it reaches almost to my elbow. I'm shaking so hard the plastic rattles like a magazine on a windy day. "Reach inside," Florence had instructed.

Ruby bleats. Her head hangs down. She's tired. And if I don't do something, her lambs will die inside her before they're even born.

Florence says I have clever hands that learn quickly. I

hope she's right. I place both hands over my heart, struggling to breathe evenly. "Okay, Taylor, you can do this. Seriously."

OMG. OMG. OMG. I slide two fingers in, wincing at how tight the passage is, then inch my fingers along the left side until I hit something. What is it? I can't tell with just two fingers. Erk. I'm going to have to put my whole hand in. "Clever hands, clever hands," I whisper. "If Florence were here, she'd say I have clever hands." I snort softly. If Florence were here, she'd be delivering the lamb.

I slide my whole hand in and feel around. "I don't know what this is." I start to panic, then remember Florence's advice. I close my eyes. I take a few deep breaths and start moving my fingers. That might be a hoof. I follow it up to a knob. That might be a knee. The back of my hand brushes against something. The underside of the lamb's neck. The lamb's right there, ready to come out, but the leg is locked on the side of the doorway. Eyes still closed, I work my hand back to the hoof, lift it gently and move it into the doorway.

I slide my hand out and open my eyes. A little black hoof. Right under the nose! "Okay, okay. You can do this." I go back in and feel along the right side. Another hoof. I move it into the doorway, then pull my hand out. One nose and two hooves!

Suddenly the head is out. Whoa! The lamb's about to be born right into my lap. I fling myself back and roll in the straw as the lamb exits with a wet splosh, soaking wet and looking dead.

"It's out! It's all wet. It's not moving. What do I do?" I yell this even though I'm alone. I need the blue bulb in the bucket. I grab the bulb and a towel, but Ruby turns and begins vigorously licking the lamb's face. It sneezes, sputters, and lifts its head.

"You're alive!"

Ruby cleans off the lamb's face, licking so hard that the soggy little body rocks. The lamb seems to be all spindly legs. When Ruby nickers deep in her throat, the lamb responds with a tiny, high sound.

I should be awed by the miracle of birth, but my heart is pounding like a jackhammer. The baby looks weak. It leans into Ruby's tongue, offering itself for cleaning.

It's so tiny and so slimy.

A pool of blood appears in the straw by Ruby's back legs. I hope this is normal.

Ruby suddenly stops licking, bleats once, and walks away, revealing another set of hooves coming out of her body. "Okay, here we go again." But the first lamb is still wet and has begun shivering. I gingerly rub the lamb with two fingers and a towel. What if it gets too cold in this October weather? Bolder now, I towel off its head, then its back and legs, going through two bath towels. "Gross, gross, gross," I mutter. The lamb is still damp but at least the slimy stuff's gone, most of it now on my overalls.

I'm so focused on the lamb that I forget about Ruby

until there's another wet splosh. Ruby begins cleaning the face of a second lamb. This one is all black.

She licks for about thirty seconds, but then she stops and steps back. The black lamb's head drops weakly onto the straw. Ruby looks at me and bleats.

"What?" I lean closer. Ruby stands there and the lamb jerks once, then doesn't move.

Something's wrong. Ruby's stopped licking it. What if the lamb's dead? I grab a clean towel as Ruby turns, revealing yet another set of tiny hooves. "Not another one!"

I pull the black lamb close, squeeze the blue bulb, stick the end up one nostril, then release it. The wet sound means I've sucked some fluid into the bulb. I do the second nostril, then both of them again. Still nothing. I rub the lamb and rock it hard in the straw. Suddenly it coughs and lifts its head. It's alive! I clean off the rest of the lamb as it looks around, bewildered.

By now the third lamb has been born and Ruby is cleaning it.

I glare at the ewe. "Don't even *think* about having another one or I'll never speak to you again." Something bumps against my thigh. The first lamb, trying to stand, has fallen against me. I pick it up, feeling its tiny little heart pounding against my hand, and place it on its feet. The lamb wobbles but stands on its own. One step, however, and the lamb tumbles to the straw before I can catch it. The lamb flails its legs until it finds its footing and tries again.

I sit back. All three lambs are alive. Ruby is cleaning

them. I feel so weak, I actually lay on my side in the straw for a few minutes.

"Hello? Taylor?"

I sit up. Caleigh's walking into the barn carrying a flashlight, her face red and sweaty. "Your mom must have come home," I say. "Thanks for coming."

Caleigh shakes her head. "Mom's not home. I walked."

My jaw drops. "Three miles?"

"Took me almost an hour, but it feels longer in the dark." She climbs into the pen. "Oh, Taylor, look at what you've done. Triplets."

Three babies, all alive. I lean against the barn wall. "What do I do now?"

Caleigh kneels beside me in the straw. "Let Ruby take care of things. The lambs need to find her udder."

"This is the first lamb born." I point to the white one standing with its legs sticking out like the poles of a swing set. "The black lamb came out next. I had to help him breathe."

"Wow," Caleigh says. "That's amazing."

The black lamb is smaller but manages to stand up thanks to Ruby's constant nudging. The third lamb, white with lots of red-brown spots, has gone straight from soggy in the straw to dry and standing on its feet, crying for Ruby.

"When a lamb starts to nurse, watch its tail," Caleigh says. "If it starts wagging, then the lamb is drinking."

Ruby is calm as she licks and nudges her babies until all three are nosing under her wooly body in search of milk. Ruby's wool is so long we can't see what's going on underneath, but suddenly the big white lamb starts to wag its tail. Then the black lamb on the other side of Ruby begins wagging. The third lamb noses around until it pushes one of its siblings away. Tail #3 begins wagging. I smile. "They're already fighting over the best spot."

"Don't worry. Ruby will have enough milk for all of them. Do you have any molasses?"

I find a bottle in Mom's lambing box and hand it to her.

"Good. I'll add some to Ruby's water. She's been working hard, so a little sugar will give her some energy." Caleigh pours molasses into Ruby's water. The thick, dark syrup turns the water brown, but Ruby sucks nearly half of it down in a few gulps.

I can't stop watching the lambs. They've dried off, and their round black eyes drink in everything. Their ears stick straight out from their heads like little fuzzy windmills. Their long legs support them better every minute, and one of them even hops once. The little movement is so sweet and happy that I can't breathe for a second.

"You look as tired as Ruby," Caleigh says.

"I know we should go inside and wait for Mom and Dad to come home, but I can't bear to leave the lambs."

Caleigh laughs. "I left a note for my mom, but it's going to be awhile before she gets home. Let's sleep here."

"In the barn?"

Caleigh snoops through a gray metal cabinet by the barn door and finds two old wool blankets. Then she uses the pitchfork to remove any hay covered in slimy stuff. While she puts down fresh straw over those spots, I call Dr. Muscato and leave another message, telling him he doesn't need to come after all. "I took care of everything," I report, amazed to be saying this. I call Mom and leave the same message.

After Caleigh makes two straw piles in one corner, I shut off the lights and in the moonlight streaming through the open doors, I find my way back to the pen. When I finally sink into the straw, instant warmth spreads through my arms and legs.

"Thanks, Caleigh. I really appreciate the help."

"No problem. I love doing this stuff." She throws her blanket over her legs, and I do the same with mine.

I take a deep breath. "I'm really sorry about the other day, and about the 4-H joke. When I'm discombobulated, I can be kind of a jerk."

"Discombobulated? Great word." She pauses. "It's okay."

The lambs nose at my boots. One stands with its sharp hooves on my shoulder and leans into my face, its black eyes curious. Another stands on Caleigh's stomach, and she giggles. Two hours ago these lambs were deep inside Ruby's belly and now they're using us as their playground. I try to stay awake so I won't miss a thing, but when the lambs go off to investigate Ruby's udder again, I pull the blanket up under my chin.

Soon Caleigh's breathing evens out, and I slip into a deep sleep. The population of McNamara Farm has increased by three.

I wake up bathed in moonlight, but my eyes don't want to open. I'm warm and relaxed and weirdly happy. I'm lying on my back. Caleigh has flung her blanket off and is sound asleep. I'm still amazed that Caleigh walked three whole miles down a dark road, with nothing but a flashlight, to help me. I start to fall asleep again, but realize that I can't move my legs. I sit up.

Caleigh is on my left, but Ruby's on my right, lying close beside me, warming me from hip to knee. Curled up on top of Ruby, sound asleep, is one of the lambs. The other two must have started there, but they've slid off and are now curled up like puppies on my lap.

How can such small animals give off so much heat? The lamb on Ruby shifts, stretches, and like thick honey, flows onto my lap until it's draped across my knee like a floppy doll. The lamb sighs and falls back asleep.

My throat tightens. The huge white moon. The smell of clean straw. The warm lambs on my legs. If I could choose one moment to remember for the rest of my life, it would be this moment.

CHAPTER TWENTY*SIX

T HE NEXT TIME I WAKE UP, IT'S LIGHT OUTSIDE, BUT JUST barely. People are speaking softly beside the sheep pen. My back hurts, which is when I realize I'm sprawled out on my stomach in the straw. Something is sucking on my ear and two other somethings are standing on my back with sharp little hooves. All of it tickles.

"Ouch." I spit out a piece of straw. I pull my soggy ear from a lamb's mouth. The black lamb noses along my face, tickling my cheeks so much I giggle, and the lamb leaps back. The other two jump off me and onto Caleigh. She sits up, rubbing her eyes.

"Hey, sleepyheads," Mom says. Mom and Dad and Caleigh's mom are standing in the barn's center aisle. Dad has a bandage across his forehead.

"Dad, are you okay?"

"Of course I am, Mrs. Beasley. I'll have two dough-nuts and two coffees to go, please."

I roll my eyes and stand. "You're fine."

All three adults climb into the pen and each picks up

a lamb. Mom cuddles the black one against her face. When she looks at me, her eyes are wet. "Taylor, I am so—." Her voice breaks up and she waits a minute. "I am so *proud* of you."

I swallow hard. "Ruby did all the work."

Caleigh stretches. "Mom, you're just coming now to pick me up?"

Her mom smiles. "No, I came about midnight but you were sound asleep, and you looked so comfortable, I decided to come back this morning."

"Hello?" Two more people enter the barn. It's Megan and Mr. Zink. "Sure hope you folks don't mind us barging in like this," Mr. Zink says, "but Megan tells me you had some excitement last night." Megan stands behind her grandfather. "I see you've got yourself a fine set of triplets!"

After all the introductions, Caleigh's mom nods to her.

"Gotta go," Caleigh says.

I surprise her with a hug. "Thanks again."

Megan says "Hi" to Caleigh as she passes, another surprise.

Mr. Zink picks up the nearest lamb and looks it over. "You got yourself a good, healthy animal here. And it's got a nice belly, so Mama here's doing a great job." He examines the other two lambs. "Three ewe lambs. Good for building your flock."

Mom claps her hands. "I didn't even think to look. All girls?"

"Yup. You got yourself some fine breeding ewes."

I exchange a glance with my parents. No one tells him we're moving.

Mr. Zink nods toward Pearl. "That one looks about ready to pop." He kneels in the straw and begins gently touching her side, then he pats her udder. "This girl's got herself an udder. Won't be long now."

More lambs on the way.

I wonder who will care for all of them when we're gone.

CHAPTER TWENTY·SEVEN

AFTER MEGAN AND MR. ZINK LEAVE, MOM LEADS RUBY outside by a rope. Dad and I follow with the lambs, and Mom ties Ruby to a tree. The ewe lowers her head to graze. When we put the lambs down, the black lamb leaps straight into the air. The little spotted one follows, staggering when she lands, then the largest one does the same. Soon all three hop and twist, clearly delighted with how their bodies move. We sit in the shade beneath a big maple tree, watching them play. They run, stumble, and hop to their feet again.

When the lambs finally get tired of running around, Mom cuddles the black lamb against her chest. "Look how tight and curly her wool is."

I run my hands along the lamb's back. "It feels like a carpet."

Mom gives me a funny look. "We can't name them, you know. We'll get too attached."

"That's okay. You shouldn't name what you aren't going to keep."

Later the three lambs skitter over to Ruby for a drink. When the black one finishes, licking the white foam on her lips, I pick her up. Her belly is so full it feels like she's swallowed a softball.

"What are we going to do?" I finally ask, stretching out my legs so the lambs can climb on them.

My parents look at each other. "You mean about selling?" Dad asks.

I nod. "Are we really going to?"

"We've already decided," Mom says.

Dad gives me a long look. "Do you want to stay?"

"I don't know. Sometimes I do. But you guys work all the time. Farming is dangerous. And up until the last few days, Dad's always been gone."

"Maybe I could keep working from home a few days each week," Dad says.

Mom sighs and considers the lamb that's fallen asleep in her arms. "I never imagined farming would be so hard."

I lay back in the grass, not minding the prickles along my skin. The big white lamb stands above me, looking huge. For the first time in weeks, life feels almost normal. *I* feel almost normal.

Dad finally gets up. "Time for lunch. These babies are full, but I'm starved."

As Mom unties Ruby to lead her back inside, a big red Buick pulls into the driveway.

Florence! I run to greet her. She climbs out and gives me a hug.

"You're not mad at me for skipping school?" I ask.

"Don't be silly." She sees the lambs over my shoulder. "You did it."

"Yes, I *did*."

Dad gets a lawn chair for Florence while I pick up the black lamb. "I helped this one breathe when she was born."

Florence accepts the lamb from me and folds it into her arms. "Didn't I tell you? Clever hands. I am so proud of you."

She looks at Mom and Dad. "I'm proud of all of you. Three brand-new babies. You've brought new life into the world. And the place looks lovely. You've been repairing things, I can tell. You've done a fine job, and trust me, things will get easier and easier. In another month or so, you'll feel right at home."

If Florence has seen the For Sale sign, she's ignoring it. My parents and I look at each other as Florence drapes the lamb over her lap and strokes its back. "Oh, what a lovely beast. These lambs are perfect. What are their names?"

Mom clears her throat. "We can't really name them, since we're not—"

"Oh, don't be ridiculous. They need names! You can't let them go one more hour without naming them. I like themes when it comes to names. Ruby's a gem, so you could name the lambs after precious stones."

Once again, my parents and I stare at each other. No one says anything, but it's amazing. Something electric passes between us. Suddenly we're all communicating without words, not just Mom and Dad, but me too. And what we say with our eyes is the last thing I expect from any of us.

I lick my lips. "Mom, Dad, what do you think? Should we name the lambs?"

Mom and Dad exchange a glance. "I'm not sure," Mom says.

I take a deep breath. "Well, if I were going to name this black one, I'd name her Onyx. Grandma McNamara once sent me an onyx necklace from Mexico."

"Onyx," Florence says. "Perfect. What about you, Michael?"

Dad shoots Mom a panicked look, then he picks up the big white lamb. "I guess Crystal would be a good name for this one."

"I love it. And the last one?"

Mom grins like a kid who's been given a barn full of toys. "This little one has some rusty orange, so maybe Amber?"

Florence throws her arms up as if we've all made touchdowns. "You are a family of excellent namers."

Dad brings us lemonade, and we drink and talk and watch the lambs. I feel full, like I've eaten a really great meal. We've decided, the three of us together. And we didn't say a word. Amazing.

Florence asks me to get a plastic bag from her car. When I return, she removes something wrapped in blue tissue paper and hands it to Mom. "I saw this in a Madison gardening shop. I think you might need it."

Mom opens the bag and pulls out a white, long-sleeved T-shirt. On the front a girl is watering her flower garden, and underneath it says, "Bloom Where You're Planted." I start laughing and almost can't stop. Florence tells Mom that sometimes it takes awhile for the blooming to happen, so she needs to be patient. Mom doesn't even recognize it's the same as my old chore shirt. She's too busy trying not to cry.

Florence hands me the plastic bag. "I found these in Madison yesterday and I knew you had to have them. I hope they fit."

I open the bag and pull out a pair of barn boots. But they aren't mud brown. They're sky blue, with orange and lime green flowers scattered all over them. My mouth drops open. They're barn boots, and they aren't ugly. "They match the yarn we dyed!"

Florence looks pleased. "Now you must learn how to knit, so you can knit a matching hat and mittens."

"Thank you!" I leap to my feet and slip on the boots. They fit perfectly.

A sheep bleats inside the barn. We fall silent. It's Pearl. She bleats again. Mom looks at Florence, who nods. "Yup, that sounds like a sheep in labor."

Mom leaps to her feet. "More babies!"

I hold up my hands and take a step back. "It's your turn now."

Mom shoots toward the barn, with Florence not far behind. Dad and I gather up Ruby's lambs and we lead Ruby back into the barn. At the entrance to Ruby's pen, I hesitate. There's sheep poop in the straw. These barn boots are so pretty and clean that I'm not sure I want to get them dirty.

But then, that's what barn boots are for, right? I step into the pens and set down the lambs. Onyx gives a little hop, squats, and pees on my brand-new barn boots.

Erk.